Tad bounces around in time and watches mankind grow and change. He loves humanity and helping when he can. However, his job isn't conducive to helping people—he's an Angel of Death.

Doug is a fun-loving drama queen. He's an amazing drag queen and hairstylist with big dreams, but despite his witty exterior, he has a dark history and is prone to self-destruction.

When Tad pushes the boundaries of his duties too far, his wings are stripped away from him, and he is sent to New York City to live as a human. Lost and alone he ends up meeting Doug, and they start a friendship that shapes them both and may last a lifetime. But nothing is simple when you're dealing with a former Angel of Death and a Drag Queen. Could these two cause the fabric of our world to collapse or will they manage to keep the future as it should?

TAD

M.D. Neu

A NineStar Press Publication

Published by NineStar Press
P.O. Box 91792,
Albuquerque, New Mexico, 87199 USA.
www.ninestarpress.com

TAD

Printed in the USA
First Edition
September, 2019

Print ISBN: 978-1-951057-40-4

Also available in eBook, ISBN: 978-1-951057-39-8

Warning: This book contains sexual content, which may
only be suitable for mature readers, explicit 9/11 details,
depictions of attempted rape, and homophobia.

For my friends who wore heels and no longer join us: Miss Ivanna Doya, Krystal Chandelier, and Miss Vinna Las Vegas, this book is for you.

Crislyn,

Enjoy the story!

Have fun with the

Angels & Queens

M. D. Mu

Prologue

WALKING BETWEEN THE past, present, and future, seeing what I've seen, isn't for everyone.

One day, I can be in San Francisco on October 17, 1989. On another—well, it was longer than a day, more like half a year—I was in Petrograd and Moscow from March through November 1917. That was a busy time. On my favorite day, as tragic as it was, I was at Alpha Base, Mars, on September 21, 2051. There was so much hope and heroism on Mars that day. I'd go back and relive it anytime.

When I think about all I've seen, in the grand scheme of the universe, it's not even a blink of an eye. However, what I've been left with is one overlying thought: humanity is amazing.

No matter what happens, humans keep moving forward. Humanity is a joy to witness and be a part of. Even in my own small way.

Humans here—at this time—aren't much different from in other realities.

I've been to three. There are more, but I'm still pretty new. In one, mankind has paranormal creatures living among them. The humans don't know it, but they are there, living and working together. I wonder what would happen if the humans on that world knew about the paranormal creatures in their midst? Something like that would be up to the Fates to decide. Which is way over my pay grade. I doubt I'll find out, but anything's possible.

On another alternate Earth, aliens have arrived. The good kind. That has been an interesting scenario to witness. I'm not sure the humans in that dimension were really ready for aliens, but they didn't have much of a choice. The Arches and Fates were working overtime there, and I'll admit, considering how bad it could have been, well, it turned out pretty good for both the humans and the aliens. At least from what I've been told and seen.

The last reality I've witnessed so far has none of those things. It's the Earth I'm on right now. The one where my work takes me today. These humans still accomplish great things, but they're alone, at least as far as I know.

A loud blare of a taxicab's horn shifts my focus. I checked the street with all the people and traffic. This is such a busy and noisy place. I don't understand how anyone can think.

Ah, well.

As much as I'd like to, I don't get to spend all my days bouncing between realities. I've heard from my brothers and sisters there is an Earth where magic and dragons exist. That would be pretty neat to see. Maybe another time. Today, I have a job to do, helping the dead. Unfortunately, I can't always interfere with history, especially if the event is a major convergence point. You know, something like the Black Death, or the fall of the Roman Empire, something hugely important to human development. So, I can't stop a dictator from rising. I can't keep millions from dying. But I can help those who die cross over and make their journey painless.

Sometimes, people don't want to leave, and who am I to tell them they have to go? Yes, it's upsetting, because I know the suffering they are going through, and I can help them, but I can't force them. Some think they have unfinished business, and that might be the case, but not for all of them. Those spirits don't want to let go, and they think staying is better. It's not. But I let them stay. I will, however, come back and check on the lingering deceased from time to time. Most souls eventually come around and let me help them. That's always a nice feeling.

To date, I've never lost a single soul. Everyone I'm responsible for gets crossed over, maybe a little late, but they still get to where they are supposed to go. Not many of my brothers and sisters can make that claim. Maybe that's why I'm able to get away with messing with fate and altering the timeline.

Inhaling the fall morning air brings back so many memories. I wish it could always be like this. It can't, of course. Without the sadness and the pain, humans wouldn't know how to celebrate the happiness and the pleasure.

I check the sky. Nothing yet.

Sitting on the park bench, I adjust my arms, flexing my wings as a pug trots over to sniff my feet. The dog's caregiver tries to tug at the leash to get the pug to move. The man can't see me, which is a great perk of my job. I don't think most people would appreciate or understand my current appearance, but animals do. I reach down and pat her head.

I love animals. Dogs. Cats. I love them all. Now, working with animals would have been a good job to have. Helping the animals cross over. They never complain, and they're always happy to have the attention. I've heard some choose to stay and watch over their caregivers and wait for them.

Now that's dedication.

Finally, the man comes over and attempts to pick up the pug. He has no clue why she stopped. I wave my hand and she trots off, confusing the man even more. I chuckle through my exhalation.

I rest my arms across the back of the bench and sigh as I glance up at the twin buildings. I'll be honest, I've played with how many die, who dies and when, but I have to be careful. I can really screw things up, and I don't want to do that. Fixing reality is no easy task, and they never get it just right again. Too many variables, I guess. And way above my skill set. That work gets handled only by the top Arches and the boss. Anyway, the trick for me is finding the balance. Like I did in 1989.

My time in San Francisco and Santa Cruz, California, on October 17, 1989 worked out well, and I count it as a huge success. I was able to find the sweet spot, the perfect balance between life and death. All I had to do was make a few of my tweaks, and the San Francisco Giants and the Oakland Athletics were in the World Series. The Battle of the Bay, they called it. I called it a job well done. Only sixty-three people died, instead of almost twenty-five thousand. Who says baseball can't save lives.

I suppose the changes didn't affect the timeline much. Well, at least, I didn't get in trouble. I've heard punishment can be bad. So that's good.

The shadow of War flashes above me.

Right on time.

She's scary but misunderstood, like all of us. Still, my wings tighten, remembering the deaths she's caused.

I don't like to focus on my failures throughout history because there have been so many. Sometimes, there is nothing I can do. Certain moments in time only offer me small amounts of wiggle room, and humans are as bloodthirsty as they are kind.

My wings tighten again, and I scout around. It feels like there's another one of us here.

Odd.

Oh, well.

It's hard not to help, because I want to. I was created to help. We all were. I've been reprimanded—well, warned I could be put on probation or dismissed—and reminded I do help, and I do make a difference, so I should be happy with that. Leave fate in the hands of others. The Arches take care of human's fate. They ensure what is to happen, happens. It's not up to me.

I often wonder if I could be an Arch. Really play with fate, and decide more than just life and death. Decide when events happen if they happen at all, who is born when, how to alter the timeline for the best results. I don't think they have it so tough. They get to write the past, present, and future, and that gives them a lot of flexibility, but there are whispers about how they leave their positions. Some have fallen. The idea makes my wings shudder, but sadly, it happens.

Not too often.

I check the sky, not seeing anything notable yet. I wonder if the Arches are involved today? Maybe. It'd make sense. I massage the spot between my back and the base of my wings.

I can hear the Arches now when they lecture me.

"You do good work," the Arches tell me. "Be happy with your job."

And for a short time, I will be.

Then I'll watch something awful happen, like I did today, and my wings will tingle all over again.

I have to act. I have to change things. I know I'm only supposed to shuttle the dead. That's my job, but sometimes, one has to bend the rules to make things right.

Humans, you are beautiful and wonderful, so creative. Watching you come to be, I can see why some of my brothers and sisters were envious. You've got a lot, including free will. However, you didn't get everything. There were counterbalances to your gifts; limited lifespan, pain, suffering, and worst of all, in my opinion, heartache.

That is something I'll never experience, and I'd be lying if I said I wasn't a little jealous.

It makes my wings shudder to think about the amount of suffering you go through and cause throughout your short lives. Which is why, on a day like today, I bend the rules, just a little. Despite this moment of respite, it's been incredibly busy for me.

I don't expect praise or thanks, because the truth is, people are still going to die, some in awful ways. They are going to leave behind families and friends, and there will be so much sorrow. Not only for their families but for the country and the whole world. I wish I could do more for those left behind, but that is a job for my brothers and sisters.

I've done what I can. And really, a few lives continuing on won't affect the future. Today, I've made several trains run late. I've made some people oversleep. I've made mundane matters urgent for those they affect. I made a small group of airplane passengers brave and courageous. In years to come, their daring will still be talked about. Hopefully, I've done enough to make everyone's passing as painless as possible. What I've altered won't stop the events to come and my tweaks won't help a great many people, but I'm limited. This event is too important. Too painful. The ramifications will drive humans and their future to the next fixed point.

Under three thousand people was my hope, and I did it. So that is something I'm very proud of. I'm getting better at my manipulation of people and events.

I glance up at the sky and watch.

It's 8:40 a.m., and I've got to cross over just under three thousand people from three different locations. These deaths are so much less than the almost forty-three thousand it would have been without my interference. And nothing near the almost half a million people over the next two weeks from a different part of the world that will keep me and my brothers and sisters busier than we care to be. So, for the next two days, my wings will get a workout. But I'm feeling pretty good. I saved five hundred forty thousand people this time, the most people saved yet for this event.

8:42 a.m.

This is my last attempt. I stand. I've tried five different times, and I can't risk another go. Plus, I think my boss is coming around to my tricks. After today, I won't be able to come back to this day, at least not to change things, but maybe I'll come back to visit.

In the distance, I see the first plane heading for the first tower. Time to get to work. I flex my wings, stretching them out. Enjoying their heaviness before I take to the air.

My name is Death, and I'm going to have a busy day.

Chapter One

DOUG GLANCED UP at the big void where the buildings once stood.

How could anyone do that? All those people, and for what? Thank God, no one I know was there. Thank goodness, Garret's train was running late. Even from across the river, seeing the buildings fall, one minute there, the next not, awful. Not knowing if Garret was alive or dead. The not knowing was awful, and it seemed to last forever. Then getting his call when the phones were back up. It was a relief. Still, the not knowing? Horrible. How do survivors do it?

Doug shuddered. He had to look away before he started to cry again. That day. The world wasn't the same. How could it be? Would it ever be the same again? He swiped at his eyes, keeping the tears he was trying to hold back from dropping. He caught his reflection in one of the storefront windows and fussed with his spiky blond hair.

One year.

The months right after the attack had been hell for everyone. People from all over the world sent support and offered help. But New York was moving on, as it should. They already had seven different architects offering new designs to fill the empty skyline. Mayor Giuliani was doing everything he could for the city, and there was even talk of him running for president.

Doug checked his flip phone and picked up his pace. He was running late. He shouldn't have spent the night at Tim's, but leaving such a sexy guy was no easy task. Not to mention they might have partied too much.

I doubt that is even possible. You can never party too much.

There was a large group of mourners, and he had to step to the side to let them pass. He took a deep cleansing breath, pushing all thoughts from his mind, and started walking again. He rushed past the families and friends heading to Ground Zero. Now he had to hustle to make it to work. He'd gotten lucky no one he was familiar with was killed. Still, every time he thought about the attack and looked up at the twin lights filling the night sky, he wanted to cry.

Monsters.

Why President Bush didn't blow up the whole of the Middle East after the attack, Doug would never understand. Instead, the president sent troops to Afghanistan, searching for Osama bin Laden and taking out Al-Qaeda.

Just as long as they find and kill the monsters who did this to us.

Doug couldn't help but stop again and glance up to where the twin towers once stood. He quickly wiped at his eyes. "I need to get out of here." He moved over to the brick façade and leaned against the wall as more people passed him, heading to the memorial ceremony.

"So much suffering and for what?" Doug mumbled. He started walking again, taking a deep breath and trying to avoid the crowds. A woman in a dark jacket passed him and bumped his shoulder, causing him to step closer to an alley. She didn't bother saying anything; however, Doug thought she said something about his size. He caught his reflection again. He hated how everything made him feel so fat. Nothing he wore looked right on him. Even the baggy pants still made him look fat and messy. He would need to start at the gym if he wanted to continue dating Tim and keep up with his partying. He frowned.

At least I have good hair.

He played with the spikes of his hair.

"It's my fault," a gruff voice whispered from behind him.

Doug startled and turned around, but no one was there. He glanced over to the dumpster.

Sitting there, a raggedy black man, with kinky hair in desperate need of a cut and wash, stared at him. The man had the most beautiful green eyes Doug had ever seen. The rich tones of his skin really made his eyes pop, quite possibly the unkempt man's best feature. The man was in shambles, and tears streamed down his dirty cheeks.

The anniversary affects everyone.

"I did this," the man groaned through his sobs. "And now I'm being punished."

Doug wasn't sure what to do or say. Should he walk away and get to the salon? Leave what appeared to be the crazy homeless guy alone? Could he do that now that they made eye contact? Could he do that today of all days? The man needed help. The man needed a shower and clean clothes. Perhaps, if he talked to him, that would be enough...well, the talk and ten bucks.

That's what Shannon would do. Talk to him and give him money. Shannon was such a kind soul, and I need to be more like him, more like he was. To honor him. Just like my drag name. Maybe Miss Enshannon needs to be more. I need to be more.

Doug's heart ached at the memories of Shannon and how wonderful he was. When he picked his drag name there was no doubt on what it would be, but to honor someone you loved had to be more than using their name.

"It's not your fault." He knelt close to the man, still keeping his distance just in case. "It was the work of terrorists. They killed all those people, not you."

"I should have stopped them. I should have done more," the dirty man moaned.

"Oh, baby, no one could have done more," Doug offered. Some people thought the government knew about the attack beforehand and the president allowed it to happen. Doug didn't buy it. Why anyone listened to these people was beyond him, but they did. He just wished they would shut up and crawl back under the rocks they came from. They weren't helping anyone, and in the long run, their remarks and comments only hurt people more.

"Now, I'm being punished. They sent me here and took my wings," the man whispered.

Was this guy a pilot? Oh, that would be awful. I bet he was supposed to fly one of the planes, and he couldn't take it. Survivor's guilt.

"No one is punishing you. Look, it's a tough day for everyone. We all feel like we should have done more." Images of the planes flying into the towers and then seeing and feeling them collapse; even at the Paul Mitchell campus on Staten Island, they were affected. *I really need to call Garret.* Doug pulled out his flip phone and checked the time. "I've got to get to work." He stopped and peeked at the crowd of people passing by and then faced the guy. A bright smile filled his face.

I know what I've got to do. A makeover. Help this guy out.

"You want to come with me? We'll get you a shower and give you a cut. My girl Minx knows all about your hair type. It'll be fun."

What the hell am I doing? I must still be drunk from last night. Or affected by what Tim and I took. This guy might kill me. No. He's sad, and on a day like today, someone needs to be nice to him. Plus, I'm a big enough guy I can take him...

Doug extended his hand.

I hope.

"You want to help me?" The man glanced around at his filthy surroundings.

Doug nodded. "Sure. Why not?"

"Most people ignore me. Some people give me money, but they rush by." The man's voice was filled with surprise.

He stood and Doug took in this guy's build. Strong shoulders, even if hidden by a disheveled brown shirt and coat. Doug got a whiff of the funk that enveloped the man. It was a mix of... Doug didn't want to think what, and he pulled back.

Definitely a shower and some new clothes. These are getting burned.

"Well, not today." Doug dusted off his pants. "I work at a salon near Washington Square. You know it?" His face got warm. "Anyway, we can walk there and get you all cleaned up. My boss won't mind."

Or at least I hope not. Nah, the bitch owes me for helping him with his makeup the other night at the club. What a show that was. I killed it.

"Thank you." The man beamed a bright pearly smile, in contrast to the dirt on his face and clothes. His teeth and mouth were probably the cleanest part of him. What's more, there was no foul odor coming from his mouth.

Good oral hygiene. I'm not even sure that is possible, given the state of him, but thank the lord.

"What's your name?" Doug asked as they weaved through the crowd, people giving them a wide birth. "I'm Doug."

"I don't have a name."

Doug froze. "What?"

"I don't have a name." The man met Doug's gaze with his big eyes and innocent face. "They used to call me..." His gaze dropped to the sidewalk.

"What?" Doug stood watching him. A tall man with a goatee hit his shoulder as he passed. "What did they used to call you? Can't be any worse than what they've called me."

The dirty man faced Doug. "They used to call me the Angel of Death before they took my wings."

Doug let out a nervous laugh as he glanced around. There was a break in the stream of people.

Great, this guy is crazy, and I'm stuck with him. Good job, dumb ass.

Doug shook his head, studying the sky.

This is all Shannon's fault. I should have kept walking. Everyone tells me not to make eye contact with the homeless. Why didn't I listen?

Doug cleared his throat. "Well, we can't call you that. How about Angel?"

The man shook his head.

"Well, I'm not gonna call you Death, no matter how cool it sounds," Doug teased as they walked again and got to the intersection. They crossed the street, ignoring the odd looks they were getting. He was used to odd looks. He had been getting them his whole life. People needed to suck it. "Oh, I know. How about Tad?"

"Tad?"

Doug smiled. "Short for 'the Angel of Death.' Well, that would be Taod, but that sounds dumb."

The man shrugged.

"Tad it is." Doug's mouth grew into a smile and warmth rushed through his body that wasn't there this morning. It was nice. Doing something good for someone on a day like today felt like a good call. Even the stench coming off the man seemed to lessen. Maybe the man didn't smell bad after all. *Or maybe I'm getting used to it. Gross.* As long as he doesn't go all batshit crazy, he could deal with the smell, which would be fixed soon enough. He hoped.

They picked up their pace and walked in silence. Doug wasn't fully sure why he was doing this. Was it because today was such a hard day? Was it his small way of acknowledging that we all need help sometimes? Was it because the world was a massive shit hole and he wanted to make it a little better? Was he doing it for Shannon? Shannon had been so kind and sweet, never having it easy. At least Doug passed for straight, when he wanted to, which wasn't often these days. And forget it when he was onstage with his big blonde wig, big red lips, and big old fake titties. Hell, this might even be fate for all he knew.

Fuck it, who cares? I'm fierce, and Tad's gonna be fierce.

Doug pulled open the door to the salon. "Hey, girls, I have a project," he announced in his loudest, most over-the-top voice possible. "This is Tad, and we're gonna make him fabulous." He snapped his fingers and everyone in the shop froze and stared at them.

A HOT SHOWER, a trim, and a shave and Tad was the hottest man Doug had ever seen, even in those nasty clothes. He looked like a runway model with his broad shoulders, strong chest, and slim waist. And his booty was a work of art. How could anyone that crazy look that good? It just wasn't fair.

At least Tad had dropped the crazy talk, and considering what he must have been through, he was polite, well-spoken, and sweet.

He couldn't have been on the streets very long. Could he? Hell, what do I know? It's not like I talk to street people all the time. Maybe more of them are like Tad. They just need someone to be kind to them.

"Girl, we gots to find him some clothes." Minx stepped back, admiring Tad, pulling Doug from his thoughts. "He's the beautiful prize in an ugly box."

Minx did an amazing job with ethnic hair. He was a wiz. It probably helped he was mixed raced with thick black hair contrasting his lighter, more European features. Still, he had his shit together when it came to cutting hair, and it showed. Minx was an artist in and out of drag.

"I know, right?" Doug fussed around his station to see if he had a shirt or something. "Nothing I have will fit his body."

Minx checked his work station as well. Both men shared a look, then faced Tad.

Tad watched them quietly. "What's wrong with what I'm wearing?"

"They smell."

"They're ugly."

"Oh." Tad peeked down at his clothes, adjusting his coat. "This is all I have."

Minx snapped his fingers. "Dougy, go check the back to see if Miss Thing has anything back there from one of her tricks." He tapped his lips with a finger.

Doug nodded and made his way to the back of the salon. He passed the storage area with all their supplies, filled with every good product known to mankind. Across from the storage room was a washer, dryer, and sink. There was also a prep station for mixing hair color. Doug checked the door to the boss's office, and finding it unlocked, Doug opened it and carefully walked in.

The office was nothing special. A desk, a filing cabinet with a huge stack of papers on top, and a couple of chairs. On the desk was a phone and a computer. Next to the workstation was Ms. Brandy's big yellow wig and a bunch more papers.

"I'm gonna need to tease her wig out." Doug made a mental note and crossed to the closet. He peeked at the work area over his shoulder. "Ugh, I'm never going to have my office like this. Ms. Brandy can't even keep an eye on the salon from back here." He shook his head and dug in the closet for boy clothes.

Doug returned, holding a pair of jeans and a T-shirt. "I have returned victorious." He laughed. "Sadly, this is the best I could do, so we'll have to make it work." He checked the clothes, then glanced at Tad. "I hope they fit."

"I hope they're too tight." Minx chuckled and waggled his eyebrows. "Tad, honey, go to the bathroom and change." He pointed. "We can burn the stuff you're wearing after."

"But I like—"

Tad's attention bounced between Minx and Doug.

"No, no." Doug's voice had a gentle tone. "We're only going to wash them. I promise."

Even though we should burn them. We would be doing the world a favor.

"Okay." Tad took the clothes offered him and vanished into the bathroom.

Doug and Minx watched him. Once the bathroom door closed, Minx pounced.

"Girl, where did you find him? He's hot."

"On the street, crying." Doug sprayed down his station, getting it cleaned up for his next customer. Between clients, they worked on Tad once he'd showered. One step at a time, and boy, did it pay off. In a way, it was like peeling an onion, except this onion got hotter. "I don't know, Minx. Seeing him there, I couldn't leave him, and he doesn't seem crazy. Well, not too crazy. I think he was a pilot or something."

Minx nodded. "Well, I'm just glad my eleven o'clock appointment canceled."

The door clicked open, and Tad sheepishly moved forward, wearing jeans that didn't show off nearly enough, but at least they fit. And the T-shirt offered a view of Tad's strong shoulders and developed chest. In his hands, he carried his dirty clothes.

"How do you feel?" Doug took the pile of clothes from Tad.

"It's nice to be clean again." Tad ran his hand over his T-shirt, then pulled at the side of his pants. "But I'm missing undergarments."

"Girl, you don't need them." Minx rotated his hips, then bounced up and down. "Let it hang, baby, let it hang." He snapped his fingers.

"Minx, don't scare him." Doug handed Tad's clothes to Minx. "Go wash these, bitch."

"Who you calling bitch? Bitch."

Doug laughed as Minx took the clothes and vanished into the back.

"Why are you and your friend so rude to each other?" Tad watched Minx walk off.

Doug froze and focused on Tad. "We're not rude to each other."

"The words you use aren't very nice."

"Oh, that, sorry. We get carried away. Bob, our boss, keeps harping on us too." Doug's neck grew warm and his hands sweated. "Minx and I went to cosmo school together. He's one of my best friends and an amazing drag sister."

"Your what?" Tad furrowed his brow as he watched Doug.

"We do drag together. You know. Get up onstage and perform." Doug glanced around the salon. It was empty for the moment. He strutted between Minx's and his own workstation, then struck a side pose with his right leg extended out, his left leg planted firmly on the ground, and looking over his right shoulder so he could see Tad. "I'm the hot sexy one and Minx is...well, Minx is messy...hence her name Miss Messy Minx." Doug relaxed and plopped down in his station chair. "Where are you from anyway?"

Tad scanned the salon and then looked at the floor. Not answering.

"Oh, never mind." Doug waved his hand, dismissing the question. "Where I come from isn't worth mentioning either. In a couple more years, I'm gonna get out of here and move to California."

"That sounds nice. I haven't been to California in a long time."

"Really, when?"

"1989."

"Oh, is that where you grew up?"

"No. I was there for work."

Doug's eyes narrowed in bewilderment. There was no way this guy was old as he was now claiming. He was barely a few years older than Doug.

Work. Right?

"Clothes are in the washer." Minx strutted back into the main part of the salon, pounding the tile floor like a runway. "Now, what?"

"I'm not sure." Doug tapped his lips. "Lunch, for sure, after my client, but maybe tonight, he can come out with us. Might be fun."

"No Tim tonight?" Minx eyebrows raised. "You're not tired of him already, are you?"

"Never." Doug winked. "But, girl, I need the break." He fanned his face.

"I still hate you for that. It could've been me all up in Tim's hotness." Minx crossed his arms over his chest. "I should have never agreed to take your clients and fill in for you last Wednesday."

"Butcha did, bitch. Butcha did." Doug laughed.

Minx laughed as the door to the salon opened. It was Doug's client, Edna, with her big dark glasses and black poofy hair. The blue knit turtleneck hid the wattles of her neck. She walked in like she owned the place.

"Hey, Eddy, looking fabulous." Doug quickly got out of his station chair and finished tidying his station. "Have a seat, hon. I'll be there in two ticks."

"Thanks, Bubbe." She waved, peeling off her glasses. The red of her nails catching the light of the salon.

Doug pointed to Tad. "You go sit over there." He motioned to the couch. "Do you want something to drink?"

Is it too early for a shot of tequila? Isn't that what Tim calls the breakfast of champions?

"Do you have milk?" Tad asked, making his way to the chair Doug pointed at.

"Milk?" Doug repeated with an open mouth and raised eyebrow.

Of course. Milk.

Tad nodded as he sat down.

"I'll check." Minx headed to the back room.

Doug smiled and waved to his client. "I'll be right there." He turned back to Tad as he got himself situated on the small sofa.

There's something strange about this guy.

Chapter Two

STRETCHING IN THE morning light, Tad gazed out the small apartment window. The view wasn't much: a brick wall. Still, there was sunlight, and if he opened the window, fresh air would waft in. His new life here was better than it was on the streets. He hadn't felt this good in a long time. Not since before they took his wings. Meeting Doug and being shown all his kindness helped Tad out of his sadness. Every once in a while, the spot on his back ached where his wings had been attached, but even that was growing less. He missed being able to stretch out his beautiful white feathers and take to the sky. Only a scar remained.

He shuddered, hoping to never experience pain like that again.

His first year as a human had been bad. Living on the streets, seeing how humans treated each other. Even those he lived with, under bridges and behind dumpsters, would fight for what little they had. There were times when others would steal the small amounts of food Tad would get, leaving him to pick out of the garbage. Then there were those who only pretended to live in the filth so they could get money from the good people who offered it. It was a small group, but the dishonesty made it harder on those who really needed the help. During those dark times, he was happy to find the food kitchens and shelters, but even they had limited resources, so Tad wasn't always guaranteed a hot meal or a bed to sleep in.

It made Tad all the more grateful Doug found him and took him in. Doug would say it had to do with a past friend of his, Shannon: "It's something Shannon would do." But Tad knew better. It wasn't Shannon; it was Doug. He had a big beautiful heart, and Tad was becoming very protective of Doug. Tad peeked over his shoulder toward Doug's small bedroom, and a slight sigh escaped his mouth. The clock on the wall read almost eleven a.m.

Even if Doug partied too much and drank too much, he is a good person. At least he finally dumped Tim and got rid of his bad influence.

Thanks to Doug, Tad had a job working at the salon—sweeping, cleaning, and answering the phone. And he had a sofa to sleep on and food in his belly. He loved food, so many delightful things to eat and enjoy. He tried hard not to think of what he'd had to eat and only focused on the good things to be enjoyed now.

He and Doug had spent the last year trying it all. Once a week, Doug, Minx, and he would go to a new restaurant, and it would be wonderful. He wasn't afraid to try new things. Now being human, he wanted to experience it all. Some foods were better than others, but when it came down to it, anything was better than picking through the garbage. He was happy Doug had taken him in and helped him get his new life going.

Tad glanced out the window again. A woman pushed a shopping cart by. She was dirty from head to toe. He never forgot his brothers and sisters on the streets. He would give the little he had to them when he saw them, and there was a shelter close to the salon and Doug's apartment that he gave food and money, even if it meant he was a little short or hungry. He was still better off than a lot of people, and he was grateful.

"Did you have a good rest?" Doug's voice was groggy. Hungover. "Oh man, I think I partied too much last night."

The door to the bedroom closed, and Doug's soft footfalls stopped. "Ugh. Why is it so bright in here? Can you close the curtains?"

Having finished taking in the warm sun, Tad pulled the shades and turned with a smile to face Doug.

"Tad, what have I told you?" Doug raised a hand to his eyes. "Wear your underwear at least."

"No one could see and you just got up." Tad bent over and picked up the powder-blue bikini briefs Minx had picked out for him. They were a little snug, but Doug and Minx assured him well-fitting was how they were supposed to be. "I thought you liked checking out my body?" He pulled up his shorts.

Figuring out what humans want and think is very confusing.

"Okay, it was fun for the first couple of weeks, but now..." Doug shook his head and lowered his hand. His eyes were red as he squinted. "Just, please, when you get up, put on clothes."

"Sorry."

"Don't be sorry, just remember. I don't need you reminding the guys I bring home what they might be having instead of me, especially with how hot you are."

"Please, don't say that." Tad pulled on his sweatpants and then grabbed a T-shirt and slipped it over his head. "You are a beautiful person. It only matters what's on the inside. The outside is just aesthetics."

"Well, until my aesthetics are as good as yours, please wear clothes around me."

"I can't help the way I look any more than you can help the way you look."

"Sure." Doug pushed his lips together. "I just... Seeing you reminds me I need to lose about fifty pounds. I should have never quit the gym."

"You weren't happy."

"But I lost twenty pounds."

"And you were mean and nasty to everyone for five months, and the guy Tim didn't help."

"Fine." Doug crossed to the small kitchen and pulled out the wheat bread. "I'm going to make toast."

"Okay."

"Do you want some?" Doug's voice was scratchy but gradually clearing up.

"Yum." Tad moved over to the kitchenette. The walls were plastered with kitten pictures. "Can I put peanut butter and chocolate chips on it with bananas?"

"And I wonder why I have a weight problem." Doug opened the bag and pulled out four pieces. "You may. Meanwhile, I'll have a small amount of honey on mine." He scowled.

"Are you coming with me to the shelter today?" Tad leaned against the small counter as Doug put the bread in the toaster.

"I suppose. Sure. I have to be at the club by seven so I can get ready. That'll give us the whole day and my head time to clear up."

Tad might not be an angel anymore, but he still liked helping people, and Doug made it even more fun.

He owed a lot to Doug and wished he could do more for him. If Tad had any of the physical desires Doug had, he would provide Doug the kind of relationship he wanted. But after they tried, even as willing as Tad attempted to be to please Doug, neither he nor his body were into it. The first time had been the most awkward and clumsy endeavor Tad had ever experienced. They tried various things, but it was all so messy. How humans found the experience enjoyable was beyond him. The movies and stories Tad read made it sound like sex was some magical event where everything happened perfectly with little preparation or effort, but that wasn't the case.

At first, sadly, Doug thought it had to do with his physical appearance, but Tad didn't care about how Doug looked. He knew how beautiful Doug was on the inside, and that made it easy. What caused the issues the first time was Tad's lack of experience and knowledge. He never gave sex any thought as an angel. And his time on the streets was focused on survival, and not human desires. Which is why, when he moved in with Doug, he viewed the movies and read the books he did, thinking they would help for the next time. But it didn't. By the second and third time, the physical sensations were pleasurable enough, but he couldn't get into it as much as Doug. And it frustrated them both.

Tad sighed.

He missed the physical closeness; it was something he had never experienced before as an angel. The intimacy was wonderful, and sometimes even now, he considered going to Doug's bedroom and cuddling next to him, but he understood that might send the wrong message. Sex was the one part of humanity he didn't understand or care for.

Perhaps, that's why the boss created them the way he did. Physically, Tad was created to resemble a male, a very attractive male with large assets according to Doug, but nothing more. He had no physical interest for either males or females. But given he was a human now, all his body mechanics functioned as they would for any human. He had a lot to get used to now.

When Doug and he had the talk, Doug was shocked by how little Tad knew or understood. He supposed Doug thought it had to do with the trauma of 9/11, and Tad never bothered to correct him. Doug explained that a male reproductive organ would harden for no reason and remain in that state for longer than was comfortable, but eventually, they would soften again. Tad and Doug discussed self-gratification as a means to lessen the instances of his erections, but Tad had no desire for masturbation. Tad became accustomed to these physical reactions and moved on with his human life.

Tad was happy when Doug finally found others to pursue for physical release. He wanted Doug to be happy in all areas of his life. And honestly, Tad found no enjoyment in anyone taking in his physical appearance.

Tad was content to just be himself and live his life, despite his human body and its foibles.

"Did you want to come to the club?"

Tad pulled himself from his memories and thoughts. "Um."

"Oh, come on. It'll be fun." Doug nabbed the toast and passed Tad the knife, peanut butter, chocolate chips, and a banana.

"I'd like to go and watch you, but..." Tad assembled his breakfast.

"Honey, people are going to hit on you. You're gorgeous. I know you hate it, but it's going to happen. God knows I tried for months, even though I shouldn't have. I was being a selfish prick."

Tad frowned at him.

Doug waved off the frown.

Tad didn't like how hard Doug was on himself. He could have said no, but he didn't. He knew Doug would stop at once, but some of these other people don't.

"Anyway, you just have to say no and tell them to fuck off."

"But I feel bad. I should like the attention, but I don't. I should like sex, but I don't. It's not—"

"Hold up." Doug waved a finger in front of Tad. "You don't have to explain yourself to anyone. You be who you are, and fuck everyone else. They just need to back the fuck off and respect you and your space."

"I know."

"Then tell them that if someone gets out of hand."

"But I don't like using bad language." Tad spread the peanut butter on the toast. "If I wanted to do those things with anyone, it would be with you. You know that."

Doug laughed and then took a bite of his toast with honey. "Well, we all know that's going nowhere."

"I'm sorry."

"Don't be." Doug put his toast down. "It's who you are. You're not into sex. No big deal. I bet when your memories return or whatever, you'll be bouncing from bed to bed. It's a shame is all, especially with your fine-ass body." He pointed to Tad and waggled his eyebrows. "So you be your bad self, and for my sake, please just keep yourself covered. I don't want to be depressed."

"I'm—"

"If you say it"—Doug's gaze narrowed on him—"I'm gonna reach over this counter and smack that mess you call breakfast out of your hands. I was teasing. It was a joke, and I'm still not fully awake yet, and I've got a headache 'cause of all this stupid sunlight." Doug took another bite of his toast and frowned at it. "What I wouldn't give for pancakes and sausage. This sucks."

Tad closed the peanut butter, took his toast sandwich concoction, and crossed back to the couch. He knew better than to be sassy around Doug, especially when all Doug ate was toast with honey and had a hangover from the night before.

Why can't he just be happy with who he is? And take care of himself.

Tad took a bite of his toast sandwich, enjoying the salt, the sweet, the creamy nature, all on the crunch of the bread.

"Do you want some milk to go with the crap you're eating?" Doug asked, and Tad nodded. Doug poured two glasses.

"You should go masturbate. You're always happier when you finish."

"What?" Glass clanked on the counter. "Tad, stop saying things like that. I almost dropped our glasses!"

Tad glanced over his shoulder, shrugging as he chewed on his sandwich.

Doug rolled his eyes, brought Tad his glass of milk, and put it on the coffee table. "You need to learn what to say and when. I hope you don't talk to everyone this way?"

Tad shook his head.

"Thank God."

"I just want you to be happy. You deserve it." Tad took his milk from the coffee table.

Doug's face softened and a smile bloomed across his lips. "I am happy, sweetie."

Then why do you drink and do drugs? Those don't make you a happy person to be around. I blame that Tim jerk.

Tad knew better than to bring up the subject of Doug's partying. Doug plopped down on the sofa. Sometimes Tad didn't believe when Doug said he was happy. Despite all the crazy and wacky comments and the sassing with his friends when they were alone, like this, Tad sometimes noticed the tears or distance in Doug's eyes.

Tad put his sandwich down and rested his head on Doug's shoulder. "I wish there was more I could do for you. You've done so much for me."

"Well, I couldn't put you back on the street. That wouldn't have been right."

"Thank you."

"You know, it's going to be a full year in a couple of weeks." Doug glanced at Tad. "I wish you'd tell me the truth about what happened to you."

"I have."

"If you say so."

Doug didn't believe Tad was an angel of death. He didn't believe in God or follow any religion. It was sad. For a few weeks, Doug and Minx had tried to help Tad get his memory back. It didn't make sense, but he learned how crazy his story sounded, so he finally went along with whatever the boys said. Doug thought he had been a pilot and blocked out who he really was after the 9/11 attacks, but when they found nothing and no record of Tad, they gave up and just let him be. Which was nice but also frustrating. Without any identification, Tad couldn't get a real job, so instead, he worked at the salon, cleaning up and doing odd jobs for Bob who paid him cash. It wasn't bad work, and he learned a lot about humans working there. Still, if he wanted to be more help, he would need to become a real person with identification.

"I can get one of the fake numbers and identification cards," Tad said.

"What?"

"I want a real job, and I don't want to have to rely on you." Tad finished the last of his toast sandwich.

"It's fine. We're fine." Doug shifted on the couch. "You need a haircut."

"Are you sure?"

"If there's one thing I know, it's when a man needs a trim—well, and a blowjob." Doug waggled his eyebrows and smiled. "Go get cleaned up, and we'll head to the shelter. Minx and the rest of the gang at the salon put together personal-care kits for the people at the shelter. It's mostly made of stuff we were planning on getting rid of, but it's still good and will keep them clean for a little while." He smiled. "It's something right. Oh, and Bob gave me money to give the shelter. You've really had an effect on all of us. You know that, right?"

Tad smiled.

Doug reached over and wiped something from the side of Tad's mouth, then showed the bit of peanut butter and banana to Tad. "You're a mess." He chuckled. "After the shelter, we'll go and have Minx clean up your edges."

Tad stood. "Okay." He made his way to the kitchen to drop off his plate and cup, then glanced over his shoulder at Doug, sitting on the sofa and staring out the window at the brick wall. He shook his head. Whenever Doug made the silly faces or started talking about sexy things, Tad realized he was sad. He just wished he could learn how to help and where all this sadness came from.

TAD AND DOUG walked into the club. Only a few people bounced around on the dance floor; the club wouldn't come to life for a couple of hours yet. Still, "Rhythm of Love" played, and a few people danced. Most people didn't arrive until nine, when the show started, and even then, the bar didn't get busy until ten or eleven.

Tad shifted the hangers with Doug's clothes to his other shoulder. He was tired and really would have preferred to go home, but Doug loved having him here and in the audience.

It's going to be a long night.

Tad gave the bar another glance. He liked it like this. No one grabbed at him or tried to hit on him. He got to enjoy the various types of music and even dance around if he wanted, which was fun.

"Can I come and watch you get ready?"

Doug had a big dopey smile on his face. "Of course. One must witness the transformation in order to believe in it." He accentuated his comment with three snaps of his fingers. "Plus, you've got the dress and shoes." He made his way to the back of the club and the dressing area, his wig and makeup kit in hand.

Tad followed, happy he didn't have to sit out front and wait. They went through a door and headed down a hall, which was plain except for a bulletin board with photos of drag queens and paper announcements for people requesting rooms or dance lessons and others offering rooms to rent or wigs and clothes to buy. The hall led to a large room with lighted mirrors and makeup tables covered with all manner of makeup and wigs. There were ten guys all crammed into the tight dressing room. They were turning themselves into their various female personas.

"Hey, sexy," Minx said to Doug, face covered in makeup but no wig or dress on yet. Tad thought he looked so weird like this, but it was part of the process. "I got you a cocktail."

"Minx, you're the best." Doug dropped off his makeup case and sashayed over. He and Minx gave each other air kisses.

"Taddy, when you gon' run away with me?" Minx asked.

"Thank you for the trim today, Minx." Tad waved.

"Don't thank me; just run away with me. I can't keep waiting for you." Minx blew him an air kiss.

Tad laughed and hung Doug's dress on the rack. He found a stool in the corner, out of the way, and sat so he could watch.

"Girls, now leave poor Tad alone." Ivanna Doya adjusted his bra and checked the bounce of his fake breasts.

Ivanna, Tad learned, was an IT Manager at some company on Wall Street. Everyone said his job was really stressful, but Tad only ever saw Ivanna here and she—he—always seemed to be in good spirits and was one of the better performers, if anyone asked Tad.

"It's fine, Miss Doya." Tad scanned the room in amazement. He didn't fully understand the appeal, but the process amazed him. What he liked most was everyone having a great time. They were a real family, and they all treated Tad nice. Still, he stayed close to Doug and Minx or Miss Enshannon and Miss Messy Minx as they referred to themselves onstage.

They had offered to dress Tad up a few times and throw him out onstage, but spending his whole existence in the shadows made being the center of attention scary. Once he let Doug make up his face at home and was surprised with how much like a female he appeared. Still, to go through all that work, then to get out onstage and perform, in heels and a dress? Nope, that wasn't for Tad.

"Tad, did you bring the duct tape?" Doug called out from behind a screen.

"It should be with the shoes." Tad stood up, ready to search Doug's makeup kit. "Did you—"

"Got it," Doug called out.

Sensitive as the male anatomy was, it amazed Tad that these guys were willing to *tuck*. Especially considering how most men were so proud of that part of their bodies. The idea of smooshing it down and in and duct taping it to make them seem more womanly seemed crazy. And what happened if they got aroused? What if they had to pee or poo? How did that work? Tad shuddered, which caused the spot on his back to ache.

Still, these fellows tucked, and some of them took great pride in how much they tucked and how much they made themselves appear female, no matter how big or small their appendage. The one time Tad asked his questions, his only answer was laughter, and Doug patted him on the shoulder, telling him, "It's part of the mystery."

Tad stayed on his stool unless asked to get something for someone as the layers of makeup were applied. There was the layer of cover-up, then the powdering, or baking as some of them called it, and then they would contour and powder again, and then the layer of colors and the finishing touches. It took some of the guys hours to get ready. With each stroke of a brush, Doug vanished and Miss Enshannon bloomed.

"Well, how do I look?" Doug stepped from behind a changing screen.

He had on his big blonde wig and a ruby-red sparkly dress, which just touched the floor, barely exposing the matching red heels. The low neckline showed off how Doug was able to manipulate his chest to create breasts, making the female illusion better.

"You look great." Tad slipped off the stool and walked over, grabbed Doug's hand, and spun him around as usual. "Beautiful as always."

"See, girls? Those comments are why I keep him." Doug let go of Tad's hand and reached for the cocktail on his makeup station. He took a heavy sip through the straw of his drink. The others laughed and raised their glasses.

"Now, it's time for you to get out." Minx put his drink down.

"But can't I stay back here?"

"No." Doug pointed to the door. "I want you to see the show. Plus, you're my good-luck charm. When you're out there, I know I'll be fierce."

"But the—"

Doug put his hands on his hips.

"Fine." Tad tried not to frown or pout. It wouldn't get him anywhere, and he really did want to see Doug perform, which was hard to do from back here.

Someone squeezed his butt and Doug laughed. It didn't hurt, and it didn't really bother him, but he recognized this form of attention from Doug. It meant he was already drunk.

He always gets handsy when he drinks.

"For luck." Doug winked, then patted his butt again.

Tad sighed and headed out. He would try to find a quiet corner by the bar. Matt, the bartender, was nice. He chatted with Tad when he wasn't busy and always gave Tad fresh drinks when he wanted.

Tad exited the hall and was hit by the thunder of the music and the booming of the crowd. The club was packed. The lights were low and the music roared. The dance floor had half-dressed men moving about to the rhythm. Small groups of women danced together as well. Tad liked the lesbians; they always treated him nice and didn't care about his appearance.

Tad weaved his way through the crowd and found an empty spot next to the bar.

People swayed their bodies in time with the music. Some had less grace and skill when it came to dancing than others, but no one seemed to care and they were all having a good time. As the song ended, everyone cleared the dance floor. A spotlight appeared, and Ivanna Doya came out and greeted the cheering crowd.

"Club soda, Tad?" Matt said from behind the counter. He had a shaved head, goatee, and a hairy chest he liked to show off. He wore leather pants Tad thought must hurt with how tight they fit, but Matt didn't seem to mind and neither did the patrons of the bar.

"Yes, please. Thank you, Matt."

"My pleasure." Matt smiled. "You gonna keep an eye on Miss Enshannon tonight?"

Tad nodded.

Keeping Miss Enshannon out of trouble was always a challenge, and was part of the reason he didn't like going out with Doug. He would drink too much and take drugs, not all the time, but enough so Tad would have to help him home. Doug's ex, Tim, had gotten him started on all that garbage, but Doug hadn't stopped when they broke up. So, if Tad didn't come out with Doug and take care of him, sometimes Doug would bring home creepy, scary guys.

"I'll do my best."

"You're his guardian angel." Matt filled a glass with club soda.

"Not me. Not anymore. I don't think Doug has one."

Matt laughed and pushed the drink over to him. "Enjoy the show. Call me if you need anything."

"Thanks." The bubbles tickled his mouth and nose as he took a swallow. The hint of lime pleased his senses, canceling out the sweet scents of cologne and the sour stench of beer.

As the first drag performance melded into the second and then the third, more and more people crowded around the bar and Tad found himself being pushed closer to where the drag queens performed, and deeper into the shadows. Tad watched the show and waited for Doug to come onstage.

Finally, Doug came out. Some nights, he would have backup dancers, normally the go-go boys and go-go girls from the club, but tonight, it was just him doing his rendition of "A Thousand Miles." Doug really enjoyed the song and had been practicing it for weeks.

"Hey there, sexy." A tall guy with blue eyes and brown hair blocked Tad's view of the stage. "What's a hot guy like you doing alone?"

Tad took a breath. "I'm not alone."

"Oh, baby, I've been watching you all night, and I haven't seen anyone." The man leaned in, and Tad got a whiff of his sickly sweet cologne, causing his nose to scrunch. The guy whispered in Tad's ear, "What a shame." The stench of cigarette breath assaulted his nose next.

The guy's hand started to massage the front of his pants. "I've heard black guys are hung, but this is a monster. Why don't you let me help you out? Go to the back and take care of this beast." The guy leaned in and tried to kiss Tad.

Can't you just leave me alone?

The guy's fingers unzipped Tad's pants, and before he was sure what happened, the guy rubbed and massaged him with his grubby hand. All the while the bass from Doug's song banged in Tad's head.

Doug was onstage, "Miss Independent" was blaring in the background, and no one saw what was happening to him.

"Please, remove your hand." Tad struggled to get free from the man.

"What? Don't you like it? I can tell you do." The blue-eyed guy kissed Tad's neck, giving him another squeeze.

"No!" Tad tried to pull the guy's hand away. "I'm trying to watch my friend." He strained to move again, but the man blocked him.

"What's your deal? Think you're too good for me?" The blue-eyed guy tried to stroke Tad but only managed to squeeze harder, causing a rush of pain through Tad's body.

"Please, I just want to watch the show." Tad made to squirm free but couldn't. It didn't matter how big Tad was. This guy had him in such a way there was nothing for him to do. If he let the guy play with him for a little while, he would stop and go away.

Just hurry up.

Tad focused on the music and not the blue-eyed guy's sour beer and cigarette smell.

"You interested in that fat fuck up there on the stage?" The guy pointed to Doug over his shoulder. "He's a pig in a dress and no amount of lipstick can help him."

"Don't be mean." Tad labored to free himself, but the man still had his hand wrapped around Tad and wouldn't let him go. "Doug... I mean Miss Enshannon is my friend and a nice person." He took a shaky breath. "Just, do what you want and go, please." He gave in. No one had ever treated him like this before. Even the people who hit on him. Why was this man doing this? Why did people treat each other like this? Didn't they realize how much it hurt?

"Hey!" Matt's voice boomed out over the music. "We got a problem?"

"Just getting familiar with this sexy-ass guy," the blue-eyed guy said, barely looking back and still not letting go of Tad.

Tad peeked over the man's shoulder at Matt. Tad's face was warm, and he didn't know what to do. He stood there, not moving. His heart pounded in his ears and his breath was fast. Before he understood what happened, Matt was over the bar and pushed the guy away from him. Yells erupted and people cleared out of the way.

"Asshole!" Matt shouted. "No means no. Now get lost."

Tad saw how big of a guy Matt was, at least a few inches taller than both him and the blue-eyed guy.

"Hey, fuck you!" the guy snarled. "I wasn't doing anything this guy wasn't into. We're just having a good time while the freaks perform."

Matt stood between Tad and the blue-eyed guy; his powerful upper body grew from his black leather pants. If anyone was an angel tonight, it was Matt. "Get the hell out of my club."

Tad wasn't sure where to face. Fists started swinging, and he ended up on the floor with a thunder of pain blasting in his head. Next, two hands grabbed him, and he jerked away.

"I got ya, honey," Doug's voice rang out, the smell of alcohol on his breath and the stench of marijuana on his clothes.

"Minx, get his other arm."

Tad didn't recognize the direction Minx came from, but he was glad to have the help.

"Can we leave, please?" Tad asked, tears in his eyes, his voice shaking. "I want to go home."

Minx nodded to Doug. "Go ahead. Get him out of here. I'll bring your stuff by tomorrow."

"Thanks, Minx." Doug gave Minx's shoulder a quick squeeze.

"I told him no," Tad said as they moved through the pushing and shoving of the crowd. "I tried to get away. I told him I didn't like it."

"Shh. It's okay." Doug's voice was tender and soft. "I need you to put yourself away and zip up your pants. Okay?"

Tad nodded and fumbled with this pants and zipper.

"We'll go out the back." Doug ushered them both out of the club.

"I'm sorry." Tad's voice shook, and his eyes blurred, his head throbbing.

Doug stopped and took Tad's face between his hands. "You did nothing wrong. That asshole did, but Matt'll handle him, and the cops will arrest him. You didn't do anything wrong. It wasn't you. It was that jerk. Honey, you could never do anything wrong. Ever. Okay?"

Tad nodded.

"God, I can't wait to get out of this hellhole of a city."

Tad rested his head on Doug's shoulder as they walked down the street for home.

Chapter Three

AT THE SOUND of the door opening, Doug peeked over the top of the sofa after pulling his eyes away from his copy of *People Magazine*.

Hard to believe someone as cute as Scott could have killed his pregnant wife. Bastard. And I'm sure he did it too.

Tad strolled in, his normal cheerful smile replaced with a clenched jaw and thinly pressed lips. He always seemed so unhappy when he got back from class. He dropped his keys in the wood bowl on the side table under the mirror.

"There you are." Doug's voice lifted as he smiled at Tad. "I was starting to worry." He put his magazine on the couch next to him.

Tad pulled off his sweaty shirt. "Class went late." He wiped his chest with the T-shirt and draped it over his strong shoulders. He still wasn't smiling. Speaking of someone cute and sexy. Doug pushed the thoughts out of his mind. He had to be here for Tad, who was upset.

"What happened?"

Tad massaged his knuckles. "I knocked my sparring partner to the mat, gave him a bloody nose." He crossed over to the small kitchenette, grabbed some paper towels, and opened the freezer. He pulled out some ice cubes and put them on the paper towel, his gaze barely leaving the floor. He wrapped up his bundle and held it to his hand.

"Oh, wow! Is he all right?" Doug chewed at his lip to hide the smile.

With a body like his, of course you're going to knock people on their butts. Maybe even a few will throw their legs in the air as well.

Doug forced himself to concentrate. Now wasn't the time to make fun.

"Yeah, he laughed it off, but I..." At the sink, Tad put down the paper towel of ice and filled a glass with water. "I wish you were there." He gulped down his drink and refilled the glass.

Doug leaned back on the sofa. "Oh, honey, where I grew up, I had to learn to beat the shit out of people early on." He lounged, picked up the magazine, and started to flip through.

There has got to be something better in this issue than the Laci Peterson case. Oh, Kevin Costner's wedding. Perfect.

"You grew up in a small town near Otisco Lake with a population of 8,000 people. I doubt—"

"And every one of them wanted to kick my fat ass." Doug sighed. "Until I started fighting back." He put down the magazine again and examined his nails. "I need a manicure."

Tad crossed over to the couch. "I hate fighting."

"I know, baby, but you need to be able to defend yourself." Doug moved his feet so Tad could sit. He patted the sofa. "Oh, I have news. I heard they picked this architect from Norway to design the performing arts and museum complex at Ground Zero. I saw the design. It's really pretty."

Tad shrugged, picked up the paper towel and ice, and crossed to the small living room.

"Taddy, it's been three years. I thought you'd be happy with the news. They're finally moving ahead with construction." Doug rested a hand on Tad's leg and shook it. "It'll be nice to have something in the void—it's so empty."

Tad sank into the couch, leaned his head back, and rested the ice on his hand. He sighed. "I am happy. But it's still hard."

"Because you lost your wings." Doug tried to hide his smirk by scratching his mouth and pretending he had an itch.

Tad scowled, held the paper towel in his sore hand so he could pick up the magazine from under his leg, and smacked Doug with it.

Doug pushed his arm, trying to lighten the moment. "Hey, sorry. What you want for—"

There was a sharp knock at the door.

"Ugh." Doug got to his feet. "Do you wanna order Chinese for dinner? I could use some pot stickers and moo shu." He crossed to the door, then glanced in the mirror on the wall, fussed with his hair, pushed his lips out, and rolled his eyes. After a minute, he opened the door.

What are the odds it'll be Jude Law here to take me away from all this?

A man in a dark-gray business suit stood there, holding a briefcase—*Nope*. He looked as unhappy as he did old. Doug wasn't impressed and would have closed the door, but he was raised better. Not much better, but still better.

"Can I help you?"

"Are you Douglas Jefferson Porter?"

What the hell! No one uses my full name.

"I'm Doug."

"I'm Mr. Daniels. I work at Sullivan & Rothschild," Daniels said. "Rothschild represented your parents, Allen and Maribeth Porter. May I come in?"

Doug's heart picked up its pace as his stomach lurched. *This can't be good.* Doug nodded and stepped aside. "What's going on?" He frowned and crossed his arms.

Mr. Daniels moved into the apartment. Tad quickly pulled his dirty shirt back on.

"Mr. Porter, is there someplace private we can speak?" Daniels asked with a tight frown.

"What you have to say to me, you can say in front of Tad." Doug rested a hand on Tad's shoulder. "We're family."

The disapproval dripped off Mr. Daniels just like it had his parents. Intolerant people like him had no place in this world.

Fuck this asshole. Believe what you want. I hope you picture us fucking. Damn, I wish Tad had kept his shirt off.

"Very well. As I mentioned, my firm represents your parents and their estate."

"And?" Doug tried to hold the growl of his voice back.

"I'm here to inform you your mother passed away in March of this year and we need to settle her estate."

Doug crossed his arms, holding himself. He took a deep breath as he continued to watch the lawyer. *Whatever reaction this man is expecting, I'm not going to give him. The people weren't really parents, not in any real sense of the word. They would have tossed me to the curb if that wouldn't have caused a bigger scandal than what was already going through the town.*

Mr. Daniels rested his briefcase on the edge of the sofa, then opened it to pull out papers. "You've not been an easy man to track down."

"Well, they weren't easy parents to have." Doug strained to keep his voice level.

There was deadly quiet in the room. The slam of a door from the apartment above broke the awkward silence. Doug spared a glance at Tad, whose stare bounced between Mr. Daniels and him.

"I'm so sorry." Tad gazed up at Doug like a sad puppy, his eyes big and green.

Doug understood Tad was trying to break the tension. He was good at that, but he didn't understand. No one did. "Don't be. I've been dead to them for years."

"But she was your mother?"

"Taddy, don't." Doug raised his hand and shook his head.

Mr. Daniels cleared his throat. "I have these papers for you to sign if you don't mind."

"Fine."

Mr. Daniels handed Doug several documents, and he read through them, ensuring he hadn't been royally screwed over by his parents. He knew his mother wouldn't do that, but he needed to make sure. They were about his parents' trust and will. He had seen them so often as a kid he understood enough without the need to dig deep into them. What surprised him was his parents had kept him in the will.

I guess it was either me or the government. Nice to know I rate higher than Uncle Sam.

"We'll close out her accounts." Mr. Daniels flipped through the papers. "Would you like us to mail you a check, or would you want to come to the office?"

"Call me, and I'll come pick it up." Doug scowled. "I've got the perfect outfit." Doug curled the ends of his lips up and his gaze narrowed.

My green strapless cocktail dress. I'll wear my red wig and the feather boa to match. A final fuck you *to good old Mom and Dad.*

"Anything else?" Doug gave an evil grin.

"I'm terribly sorry for your loss."

"You mean you're sorry for the loss of their retainer and all their money," Doug corrected.

Mr. Daniels's face got red, but he said nothing and strode to the door where he stopped. "I'll call you in a week or two. Here's my business card."

Doug took the offered card and stood there. "Goodbye."

"Take care, Mr. Porter." Mr. Daniels turned, his expensive silk suit making a swishing sound.

The lawyer barely cleared the threshold before Doug closed the door.

Doug ran a hand over his mouth and tossed the card on the table by the mirror. He quietly made his way into the kitchen and opened the top cabinet. He pulled out a bottle of tequila and unscrewed the lid, not bothering to get a glass, and took a big hit.

"Doug?" Tad met Doug at the counter. His eyes were still as large as a puppy's and his expression was a mix of pain and sorrow.

"Don't start on the drinking, Tad. Those bastards killed Shannon, you know?" His face was hot and his eyes damp.

I want to get shit-faced and then stoned. Then find a guy to suck and fuck.

He leaned in a little closer to Tad.

I should give Tad another go. No. I can't. He's too innocent.

"Who?"

"Shannon," Doug barked out. "The hellhole I grew up in. Those miserable eight thousand assholes." He met Tad's gaze for a second and then glanced down at the counter. "Shannon was so sweet and tender. Like you. He couldn't throw a punch or fight to save his life. He hated fighting. He was beautiful and kind. A skinny thing, but adorable."

Tad leaned on the counter, biting his lower lip and saying nothing. That was the thing about Tad. He never interrupted. He let Doug talk and vent when he needed to.

Doug took another drink from the bottle. "We talked about moving to California, him and I. Together. To get away from all the hate in town. People can be so cruel, even now, but it was worse back then. Anyway, he wanted to go with me to the prom." He glanced over at Tad. Those beautiful green eyes and how sweet Tad looked reminded him so much of Shannon. "Me. Can you believe it? He wanted to take my fat, ugly ass to the prom."

"Doug." Tad frowned.

Doug pressed a finger to Tad's lips.

I know what I am and what I look like.

Doug cleared his throat. "Anyway, that was all Shannon wanted. His only sin. But in Clearwater, nope. No gays lived in that whitewashed picture-perfect town." He took another pull of tequila. "When I asked my parents if I could go with him, well, that was the gay straw that broke the camel's back. They forbade me from not only going to the prom but also from talking to Shannon anymore."

"Why does it matter who took you? Who cares?" Tad scratched his head.

Doug laughed. "It sure as shit wasn't some happy sappy *Queer as Folk* TV moment where Brian shows up and surprises Justin." He shook his head. "They called Shannon's folks and told them to keep their homosexual son away from me. They were so clueless." He laughed again. "Shannon showed them. Showed them all. On the night of the prom, he got all dressed up. I'm sure he was beautiful." He took another drink from the bottle. "Shannon climbed to the top of the gym, tied a rope around his neck, and jumped. Right in the middle of the dance."

The memories were from the days after. "All the false crying and weeping. All the kids who teased him and hurt him crying and saying what a great guy he was. They were as fake as the rest. The only honest people were the ones who said Shannon would rot in hell where he belonged." Doug took another swallow. "Of course, they didn't say it too loud. But, you know, at least I could respect them because they were honest, not only with their actions, but with their words. Unlike everyone else who pretended to mourn. They didn't know him. They didn't care."

If they did, Shannon would still be alive.

"That's why I use his name for my drag name. The night of his death *Miss Enshannon* was born. I swore, I would never let those fucking monsters forget him. Every time they saw me dressed up, they would be reminded of him. Especially my parents. If they would have only let me go with him. But I reminded them of what they did to that beautiful soul." Doug swiped at his eyes. "The purest thing Clearwater ever created, ever had."

"Oh, Doug." Tad covered his mouth with his hand. There were tears in his eyes. It appeared like a mix of pain and regret. How could Tad feel such pain for a person he never knew? It just went to show the depth of Tad's compassion. Doug could read it on his face as easily as he could read the morning headlines in the paper.

Doug shook his head. "It's fine. He got out. I was still trapped there, and like everything, there was no hiding. Sure, they tried to cover it up, but in a small town, no way."

"I don't know what to say."

"I swore I would leave that shithole as soon as I could." Doug nodded. "And I did. I came here, put myself through school, and never looked back. I kept the best part though: his name." Doug grinned. "The farther away from there, the better."

"But your family?"

"Not my family. You, Minx, Ivanna Doya, Krystal Chandelier—that's my family." Doug took another drink. "I'm gonna get my money and move. There's a salon out in San Jose, the Bay Area. I want to buy it. I'm sure it's a mess and will need a lot of work, but it'll be mine and I'll be away from here. I'll be the youngest salon owner around. Ivanna knows the owner." He faced Tad. "You'll move with me, right? Minx won't move, but you can come with me."

"I... I'm not sure."

"Please, Taddy, I can't go alone. I need to have a friend there with me. I need someone there to be my family." Doug brushed at the dampness around his eyes.

"Of course, I'll go with you."

"You're the best." Doug took another drink, finishing off the bottle. "I'm gonna own a salon, and it's gonna be fabulous." He pointed to Tad. "We're gonna be fabulous. San Jose is gonna love us."

"SO?" DOUG PUSHED open the doors of the salon with the boxes he was carrying. He was hoping for a burst of cool air. There was none. It was as warm inside as out, and the shop was stale, filled with dust and a funk that said this place hadn't been aired out in a long time. "What do you think?" Beads of sweat dropped on the box.

I thought San Jose was supposed to be cooler than New York. Ugh.

Tad peered around Doug, brushing away a few cobwebs. "It needs to be cleaned." He adjusted the boxes he was holding to one arm and fanned his face with his other hand. The sound of crumpled paper under his feet caused him to frown.

Doug put down the box and a puff of dust lifted off the counter. He sighed and rested his hands on his hips. "Girl, I know. What about the space? Amazing, right?"

"It looks nice." Tad pointed out the dusty window. "What's the strange tower thing across the street?"

"I don't know, air raid siren or whatever. I'm surprised it's still there."

Tad shrugged.

"I have so many plans. I want to give the whole place an upgrade, make it sparkle, like me." Doug spun around, raising his arms. "I'm telling you, Taddy, this shop is gonna make Willow Glen glitter."

"If you say so."

"You have no vision." He pointed at Doug. "No imagination. New York jaded you." He pulled at his T-shirt a few times, creating some airflow over his sweaty chest and back.

Tad bit his lower lip. "It's not what I remember."

"Oh, right, when you were here last...for work." Doug poked him in the stomach and smiled.

"I really wasn't here in San Jose. I was in San Francisco, Santa Cruz, and Oakland, mostly."

Doug shrugged, walked over to the lights, and flipped the switch to get a better view and turn on the overhead ceiling fans for some air. The lights flickered a couple of times before starting up and then blinking out. "Probably a loose wire. I'll need the contractor to come check all the electrical, especially for the upgrades I want to make."

"Probably." Tad glanced up. "Should they flicker?"

The lights fluttered again and, this time, stayed on.

"Yay!" Doug clapped.

He would need to buy all new equipment, fixtures, and he wanted to add an espresso bar for customers.

I'll have some fancy aroma therapy stuff. This is gonna be the place to get your hair and nails done. Screw Beverly Hills.

It was gonna be all about Doug's Salon in San Jose. Not Doug's Salon; he would need to come up with a better name. Something fabulous like him. He was going to make this town the center of beauty.

The lights flickered out again. "Oh, come on!" He headed back to the light switch and flipped the toggle a couple of times. Nothing happened. "I'm gonna check the circuit breaker box." He passed the covered chairs and the washbasins. The old-style dryers would need to go. He entered the back storeroom and found the empty space where the washers and dryers should be. "Tad, flip the switch for me."

"Okay."

Doug fumbled around, looking for the fuse box. He moved some empty boxes and pushed a shelf out of the way.

"Nothing," Tad called out.

"Well, duh, give me a minute." Doug found the fuse box and opened it. "Okay, let's see." He read through the various circuit breakers until he found the one marked lights. He switched the breaker off and then back on.

"Still nothing."

Doug shook the breaker and tried turning it off and on again. "Check it now."

The lights all turned on. A flash of light from the front blinded Doug as a loud bang vibrated the space around him. The breaker flipped with a spark, followed by a loud *thud*.

"Oh God." Doug thundered to the front of the shop. "Tad!" He rushed over to Tad, who was spread out on the floor, his eyes closed. "Tad." There was an acrid scent in the air. Doug checked Tad's hands and discovered burn marks. "Oh, fuck!"

Doug reached into his pocket and pulled out his cell phone, then flipped it open.

He started to dial 9-1-1 as Tad coughed.

"Oh, thank God!" Doug closed his phone.

Tad had a confused look on his face. "What happened?"

"I thought I killed you. That's what happened. Are you all right?"

Tad checked his hands and rubbed the burn. The skin started to flake away. "There's a problem with the electrical."

"Ya think?" Doug shook his head and chuckled nervously. "You must have gotten only a little bit of the charge. The shock could've killed you. I can't believe this. I'm so going to raise holy hell with the Realtor. I knew this place was going to need work, I mean it's an old building, but how did it even pass inspection?"

Tad coughed. "I guess I'm lucky."

"I'd say so. Can you stand?"

Tad nodded.

"We're not touching shit till I talk to the contractor, and I'm calling the agent. The inspection never said anything about faulty wires. I bet the panel is connected to the original wiring and probably not even new wiring. These old buildings are filled with screwed up shit. I should have known better. Damn it!" Doug helped Tad to his feet. "I thought you were dead. I really did. You were so still. I can't... God, Tad...you scared the crap out of me."

Tad took a breath and his gaze dropped to the floor.

"Come on, let's lock up and get out of here." Doug glanced around the shop one more time. "It's time for a drink. There's a gay bar downtown I want to try. See if I can find a sexy man and maybe score some party favors."

Tad frowned.

I know you don't approve, but it's been a long day, and I deserve it.

Doug didn't want to fight, so he kept his thoughts to himself as he knew Tad would. Doug dusted Tad's shoulder and fixed his collar. "Enough near-death experiences for one day."

Chapter Four

"OH MY GOD! Oh my God!" a man's voice screamed in Tad's ear. "I swear I didn't see him. He just walked out in front of me."

"Is he breathing?" a woman called out.

"Call 9-1-1," a man with a worried accent commanded.

"Is he dead?" a high-pitched female voice said.

Tad lay on the ground, not quite sure he understood where he was. His head hurt and the air was slow to fill his lungs, but hesitantly, he remembered what had happened. He was remembering living on the streets of New York for a year before meeting Doug and Minx that day and then moving to San Jose a year ago. And Minx's upcoming visit in a few weeks. He had been human for five years and was wondering how long his punishment would last. There was a car: a green Jetta.

I'm on the ground. I'm hurt. I've been hit by a car.

Tad carefully opened his eyes; the world was a blur. First, he caught the blues of the sky; then faces came into focus. A mix of people stared at him. Black, brown, white, male, female, so many faces. He blinked, trying to focus. His mouth and nose both were overwhelmed with a copper scent. He tried to move.

"Oh, thank Christ," a white guy said, keeping Tad from sitting up. "Don't move. We've called 9-1-1."

"I'm fine." Tad shuffled his feet. They worked, and he twitched his hands. They worked as well. Neither his feet nor his fingers had worked a moment ago. A pair of hands kept him down. "I'm okay. Really." He pushed the hands away and sat up, then focused on the green Jetta with a dent on the hood.

That's a big dent. How is this possible?

"He should be dead," a lady with blonde hair said. "I saw him fly through the air. How is he moving?"

"He's not dead." The guy with glasses and a flat nose said. "Look, he's fine." Tad noted the nervous highs and lows as the man spoke.

He nodded and stood. "I'm okay, just shaken." His body was functioning again. It shouldn't be, should it? His head cleared, and his breaths came much easier. He took in the surrounding scene. About twenty people hovered around him, and in the distance, he could hear sirens. On the street, cars passed at a snail's pace.

"I'm sorry about your car." Tad ran a hand over his torn shirt and jeans, noticing where lines of blood had been but now no actual cuts on his skin.

Is this my blood? It has to be, but where are the wounds?

The guy laughed. "I'm just glad you're talking and standing. The ambulance should be here pretty quick."

"Oh, no. I'm fine."

I can't go to the hospital. Can I? What would they find? What would they do to me?

"I don't want to be any trouble." Tad grabbed his backpack and glanced down at his clothes. The edges of his lips tugged down as he frowned.

I'm a mess. I shouldn't...but how? How am I gonna explain this?

"It's no trouble. I have really good insurance." The flat-nosed man ran a hand through his hair. He inhaled and a nervous laugh fell out with his exhale.

"I really need to go." The sirens sounded closer. "I've got to go. There's my bus." Tad pointed and pushed past the gathered crowd, hearing a few calls from behind him as he rushed over to the approaching VTA bus. He needed to get out of here. He thought he understood what was happening. No cuts, but there had been cuts because there was blood. He had healed. He hadn't been able to move, but now nothing was broken.

He walked toward the bus stop.

He should be dead and he knew it. He had seen enough death and accidents as an angel. No human, no mortal would still be alive.

So what am I? Am I still an angel, or am I a human? Or something else? What kind of punishment is this?

He started walking faster.

This whole thing was just like with the electrical shock a year ago when Doug had him toggle the light switch. The electrician was flabbergasted and said Tad must have had a guardian angel watching out for him because Tad had easily absorbed ten amps or more of electricity from the switch. He should have died then, but he hadn't. He chalked it up to luck, but today...this car accident.

I can't die. It's part of my punishment. I've heard of this but didn't realize it was possible. Why would my brothers and sisters do this to me?

Tad reached the bus and got on just before the doors closed. He paid the fare and found a seat. He inhaled and exhaled several breaths, not turning back to the scene of the accident.

What am I gonna do? What am I gonna tell Doug?

On the bus, Tad did his best to clean up. He pulled out a hoodie from his backpack and slipped it on. At least his hair was buzzed short, so it wasn't messy. He wiped at his face and the visible blood. The copper smell was gone. He had fully healed. He peeked down at his jeans. There wasn't anything he could do, but maybe people wouldn't notice. He looked up into the stares of several of the passengers, but luckily, no one said anything.

He took a shaky breath.

What does this all mean?

Tad got off the bus and checked both directions of Lincoln Avenue twice before he crossed. As he carefully walked down the sidewalk, he passed Mann's Jewelers, a unique jewelry store Doug always liked to peek in to see what they had. Tad liked tagging along and checking out all the beautiful stones and gems. Plus, he liked the watches. They had so many of them, and the *tick tocks* always made him smile because they reminded him how time was precious. As was life.

They were a good neighbor to have as well. When Doug first opened Doug's Trim and Nail Salon, he'd offered to cut everyone's hair for free for the first few months. Ever since, they referred folks to the salon. He and Doug had told people to check them out as a return favor. Tad peeked in to discover Anna was opening the wedding ring case for a male customer.

"Hi, Tad." Anna mouthed and waved.

"Hey." He returned the gesture and walked to Doug's shop.

I need to tell Doug. He's my friend and has a right to know. Especially if I can't die. What if I don't age?

Tad checked his reflection in the window and shook his head. Staying the same while living as an angel worked, but not as a human. He'd watched enough movies and TV to know how people, even good ones, treated life forms that were different, and he didn't want to spend however much time he was being punished as a test subject.

What's gonna happen now?

He glanced up at the sign of the salon. He liked the scissors and fingernail with the stylized letters, Doug's Trim and Nails. It had taken five months before the shop was ready to open, which had pushed the grand opening to early September. Doug had insisted on every detail being perfect, and it gave him time to market the shop and build up a buzz.

Doug was a savvy businessman. With the money he'd gotten from his inheritance—Tad had never asked how much—Doug was able to get what he wanted in the shop and buy a cute house not far away. He'd created a Myspace page and a website where people could book appointments. Doug really had a smart mind when it came to marketing.

Something pulled at Tad's leg, and he looked down in time to catch a dog sniffing at his feet. He smiled.

"Leave the man alone, Lady."

The cocker spaniel whined but moved when a woman in jeans and sweater pulled the leash.

Tad offered a small wave to the dog, noting he really needed to wash his hands. They were filthy from the accident.

The dog caused a tug at Tad's heart. He wanted to get a puppy, but Doug had nixed the idea, saying with the hours they worked, they were gone too long, and it wouldn't be fair for the dog or their home. Tad didn't push the issue, but he still wanted a puppy.

Life and the house weren't so bad. Tad had his own room and bathroom. The house was nice, and the location made it easy for Tad to get around since he didn't drive. Except, now walking was proving to be dangerous. He glanced down at his clothes and sighed, dusting off his pants.

If he drove, he wouldn't have gotten hit by the green Jetta today. In order to drive, he needed his green card. There were places and people who helped people like him—ha! Not really like him. He wasn't human, was he? *No.* Still, he was checking into some of these service centers.

Then I'll be able to drive.

Tad smiled.

Assuming that will actually matter anymore.

Tad frowned.

I need to clear my head.

Tad took a deep breath, cracking his neck. He opened the door to the shop, and the smell of hair dye and floral shampoo filled his senses. Terrie's, Jill's, and Paul's stations all had customers, and they chatted away, working their collective magic, making their customers fabulous. Kim had a client at her nail station. The grating sound of filing the customer's nails made him shiver.

Two of the salon chairs were not in use, and the second nail station was empty too. Fresh roses and orchids sat in a vase at the reception station, which was surprisingly empty. Off to the side was a refreshment station packed with fresh coffee and teas for clients to enjoy. Doug had promised he was going to make this salon glitter, and it did. The polished floors and the light-cream walls made every color pop out.

Tad dropped his backpack at the reception desk and strolled to Doug's private workspace. Ocean mist filled the air, not overpowering like an old woman's perfume, but the right amount. Doug had soft ocean sounds playing, which muffled all the shop noise.

Doug's private station sat at the front of the salon and off to the side, near the large picture window, so people outside could see him work. There was a private shampoo sink for his assistant to wash his client's hair when Doug couldn't do it. The location also gave Doug privacy to talk in peace with his clients.

Tad stood and watched Doug work.

"I'm not sure how much more value my house can lose, Doug," his female client said as he clipped away. "It's already dropped $150,000."

"Don't worry about it." Doug smiled at Tad but spoke to his client. "The news says the housing market will stabilize." He continued cutting. "Hey, Tad."

"Well, our neighbors, the Nguyens, are trying to sell now before the value drops any more. Two thousand seven is going to be even worse."

Tad leaned against the wall, glad to be away from the craziness of the car accident and the bus. Watching Doug work always had a calming effect on him. The hoodie covered most of his head and any possible dirt or whatever from the ground. His pants didn't look too bad, but he needed to get the worried look off his face.

At least, I don't look too awful. Still, I should be hurting and I'm not.

He frowned at the floor, not wanting Doug to see him.

"Well, you tell that sexy hubby of yours not to do anything stupid. You have to play the long game." Doug spun the woman in her chair so he could check the length and see how the style worked head-on.

The shop phone rang. Unanswered, the machine took the call.

"Tad, honey, Sue isn't here yet. Do you mind manning the phones?"

"Sure." Tad headed back over to the reception desk. "I can stay for a while, but I need to get down to Charities this afternoon." *And I want to go and change my clothes.* "I'm helping in their donation center."

"Great, thanks." Doug waved. "Now, Caroline, honey, don't worry." He pulled out the hair dryer and started Caroline's blowout.

"It's easy for you to say. You paid cash for your home." Caroline sat still, letting Doug work.

Doug stayed quiet as he fussed with her hair, making sure it set. Once he had the style he wanted, he finally spoke up. "Did you want me to do anything else? Even though Eddie isn't here, I can take care of you."

"No. I just needed to get it styled for tonight." Caroline beamed at Doug, playing with the ends of her hair. "It's amazing."

The salon phone rang again and Tad answered, "Doug's Trim and Nail Salon. How can I help you?"

"Taddy, is that you?" Minx squealed in his ear.

"Hi, Minx." Tad smiled, staring out the picture window of the salon at the cars driving by.

"I wanted to give Miss Thing a call and let her know..." Minx got quiet.

"What? What's wrong? You're still coming out, right?" Tad glanced over at Doug and then back out the window.

"Yes, I'm still coming out there, but this can't wait. It's been a few months, but I thought he should hear from me Tim died."

"That's awful."

"I know you weren't a fan of his, but Doug really liked him." Minx's voice was deeper, like the night Tad got attacked by the creepy guy at the bar. "Anyway, I just got the news. There's nothing anyone needs to do. I guess he was cremated by the city. He didn't have any family. It's awful when you think about it. So alone."

Not alone... I hope.

"What happened?" Tad didn't like the guy, but no one deserved to die alone, and that was one of the things he liked about being an Angel of Death. He was there for even the loneliest of people.

I hope the Angel of Death was kind and gentle with him.

"Overdosed," Minx said. "I thought Doug should know."

Tad nodded. "All right, I'll have him call you as soon as he's finished with his client."

"Okay. It's just so mess—"

The door burst open and a thin girl with hot-pink hair rushed in. "I'm late. Doug, I'm sorry. Some guy got hit by a car and tied up traffic, and I guess he vanished. Hi, Tad." Sue rushed to the back of the shop.

"Sorry, Minx. Sue just got here. I'll have Doug give you a call as soon as I can. See you in a couple of weeks."

"Looking forward to it."

Tad sighed. "Thanks for calling."

"Bye, sweetness," Minx said and was gone.

Tad shook his head and put the phone down. Tim's death from a drug overdose didn't surprise Tad. Perhaps Doug would reevaluate his own partying so he didn't end up like Tim.

I wouldn't let that happen to him.

Doug walked Caroline to the door of the shop. "See you in two weeks." He hugged her.

"Thanks, Doug." Caroline rushed out the door.

Doug crossed over to Tad and gave him a big bear hug, wrapping his heavy arms around his waist. "What happened to you? Did you get run over by a bus or something?"

Tad forced what he hoped was a smile, but his gaze dropped to the floor.

"What's wrong?"

"Minx called. You need to call him back, and I need to talk you about something, but not now. Tonight. Okay?"

Doug nodded, his gaze narrowed on Tad. "Of course."

"Hey, Doug, Tad," Sue said as she returned. Her breathing was back to normal, and she appeared more composed. "I'm really sorry about being late."

"You're here now, and that's all that matters. Not like someone died." Doug moved to the register and put in the money from Caroline.

TAD PACED THE hardwood floor as he waited for Doug to get home. The clock showed 10:00 p.m. He hated when Doug was this late, but Wednesday was his late night, so Tad had to wait. It gave him time to go over how to tell Doug.

How the heck do I tell him I can't die?

Doug never believed him about being an Angel of Death, and now he was going to spring this on him.

The lock on the front door clicked. Tad rushed over and opened it.

"Tad!" One hand on the doorknob, Doug got pulled into the house with the opening door.

"Sorry, I just..." Tad stepped out of the way.

"Honey, you can't do that. I could've fallen and squashed you." Doug waggled his eyebrows, a big smile on his face as he closed the door.

"I wish you wouldn't say that." Tad crossed his arms. "You're not so big that you would hurt anyone."

"Anyway." Doug waved a hand and headed over to the kitchen. He opened the cabinet and pulled out a bottle of rum. "God, I need this. I can't believe the news about Tim."

Tad pursed his lips but kept his tone calm. "Doug, I really need to tell you something."

"Let me pour my drinky. Then we can talk."

"Can we talk first?" Tad asked, trying to keep his voice as neutral as possible. "Then you can drink." He didn't want to piss off Doug.

"Don't start."

Tad huffed.

Well, that didn't work.

"Look, I gave up the drugs. Now all I do is have a drink every so often." Doug was getting flustered.

"And smoke pot." Tad didn't want to fight. This wasn't how he wanted the conversation to go. He glanced over to the living room with the sofa and chair. Maybe he should make Doug have a seat.

"Pot's not a drug, and it helps me sleep."

Tad shook his head. "I got hit by a car today," he blurted out.

"What?" Doug put the bottle down and rushed over to Tad. "Why didn't you say anything? Oh my God, are you all right?"

This isn't how I wanted to say it.

Doug ran a hand over Tad's face. He checked his shoulders. "And to think you've been dealing with this all day on your own. Oh. My. God. You should have said something."

Tad stepped back. "I'm fine. In fact, I'm perfectly fine." He took a deep breath. "I never get sick, and if I do get hurt, I'm better in a few minutes. Like today."

"You're one tough cookie."

"It's not normal." Tad leaned against the counter. "Doug, I get you don't believe my past as a former Angel of Death. I get it, but I can't die. It's part of my punishment. I have to live forever among humans." He tried to meet Doug's gaze.

"Not this again." Doug returned to the counter and poured his drink. "You have scars on your back. It's a burn, not where your angel wings used to be. After 9/11, you had a mental break, and you blocked out your memories. You probably knew people who died. When I found you on the street, you were a mess. Crying, starving, all those smells." He crinkled his nose then sipped his drink.

"Today, I got hit by a car and everyone thought I was dead." Tad ran a hand through his hair. He knew this sounded crazy, but Doug had to believe him. Today was just one more reminder of who and what he used to be. "Remember when you first bought the shop, and I got shocked. The electrician said I should have died—"

"You were lucky." Doug took another sip of his drink, finishing it off. He refilled his glass. "That doesn't make you immortal or a former angel or whatever. It's ridiculous." He grabbed the bottle and put it away. "I'm too tired for this, and I still need to work on my wigs for this weekend's show. Minx will be here next week, and I want to show her around. Maybe convince her to move west." Doug snapped his fingers. "Oh, can you go and pick up my dress at the dry cleaner?"

"But..." Tad wasn't sure what to say.

How do I make him believe me?

The butcher block on the counter was filled with knives. He walked over and pulled out the biggest.

"Tad, what are you doing?"

"Proving it to you." Tad plunged the knife into his chest—wincing at the pain—and stood there, staring at Doug. The knife stuck out of his chest.

"What the fuck!" Doug yelled, dropping his drink. The glass shattered on the tile floor.

Tad pulled out the knife and studied him. "Believe me now?"

Doug's eyes were the size of saucers as he gawked at Tad.

Tad dropped the knife in the sink and pulled off his shirt. "Now do you believe me?" The wound on his chest had a few drops of blood, but they immediately clotted and stitched back together. Within seconds, the wound was healed. Tad wiped away the blood and poked at the spot. Just like this morning, there was no mark or scar.

Doug met Tad's gaze and the color drained from his face. Doug took a step forward and touched Tad's chest, not speaking.

"Doug." Tad took Doug's hand.

Before Tad could react, Doug collapsed forward, dropping them both to the floor. Doug landed on top of Tad, pinning him to the kitchen tile.

Chapter Five

DOUG'S EYES GRADUALLY opened as he stretched out his arms over his head, the morning sun barely peeking through the curtains. The room was cool, and the air was still. He loved moments like this. He felt rested and relaxed. He sighed, not wanting the moment to end.

Memories of the night before gradually came back to him.

A dream. I drank too much; that's all.

The door opened. "You're awake." Tad brought in a tray with coffee and toast. "I've been worried about you." He put the tray down next to the bed. Tad was dressed in sweatpants and a Disney California Adventure T-shirt from their first trip Disneyland a few months back.

The rich scent of fresh coffee and buttered toast caused Doug to take a deep breath. His stomach growled in anticipation.

"I thought the smell of coffee and toast would wake you up. I can make some eggs and bacon if you want." Tad smiled.

As Doug's mind cleared, the memories of the night before flooded his head. The knife. The blood. The healing.

Was it a dream? No, it couldn't be. It was too real.

He glanced over at Tad and the warm bright smile with a hint of worry around his beautiful green eyes. "Only a dream," Doug whispered softly.

Tad's smile turned into a frown.

God. It was real, wasn't it?

Doug pulled the blankets closer to his chin as he scanned the room. Beads of sweat started on his forehead as his mouth dried. "It all happened, didn't it? It wasn't a dream. You...you're... What are you?" His heart pounded fast, and he wanted to run.

"Doug, it's me." Tad tried to reach out. The frown vanished and a strained smile tugged at his lips. "I had a hard time getting you to bed 'cause I didn't want to hurt you. I figured letting you sleep was for the best. I think you needed it."

"You stabbed yourself." Doug shook his head, trying to make sense of everything he'd seen and what Tad told him. "It has to be a joke."

"Doug, it's not a joke." Tad put his hands on his hips. "I don't want to do it again 'cause it really hurt, but I will if I have to."

"No, no." Doug waved his hands. "But it can't be real." His voice cracked. What he had seen last night was real. He readjusted his position in the bed. Tad was his friend. They'd been living together for years. They traveled together. Hell, they had even had sex a few times. "I had sex with an angel."

"An Angel of Death, there's a difference. Same with an Archangel. Although I really can't imagine them having sex. You thought I wasn't into it—"

"Stop." Doug scooted away from Tad.

"Doug, it's not a big deal. Now, you believe me." Tad shook his head and a big dopey, beautiful smile filled his face.

Doug fanned his head, and his heart continued to beat a mile a minute. Even with the chill of the room, beads of sweat rolled from his forehead. "I... I need to shower. I...how...oh God." He sat on the bed and Tad studied him with those bright green eyes of his. They always bored into Doug. *He's so beautiful. Of course, he's an angel...angel of death...whatever.* "The scar on your back? Your wings?"

Tad frowned, rubbing the center of his back. "They got taken away."

"Because you didn't stop the attacks on 9/11?" *Everything he told me is true.*

Tad's gaze dropped to the floor. "No." His voice grew soft. "Because I interfered. I couldn't let all those people die. I couldn't." His words came out quicker and tears danced in his eyes. "We're not supposed to mess around with the timeline or history, but we're given a little latitude, and it's not like I hadn't done it before. I've always tried to lower the death counts. You...you humans are amazing and your lives are so short. I couldn't do nothing. I had to help. So many people deserved to live longer. I had to. It was the right thing to do. I'm sure of it."

"So, you, the Angel of Death, saved people on 9/11?" Doug tried to wrap his head around all this. *It's crazy.* He couldn't deny what he saw, and it explained a lot about Tad. No identification, no record, no family, no nothing. "But with so many people dying that day, a few more saved lives doesn't seem bad."

"It wasn't a few. There would have been 539,670 souls the first week." Tad's voice was barely a whisper.

"How?" Doug ran a hand over his chin.

"Well, I—"

Doug waved his hands in front of him, stopping Tad. "Never mind. Don't tell me." He tossed the comforter off, almost toppling the tray with coffee and toast. Tad caught it all. Doug stood, probably faster than he should have as the room spun, but he gathered himself and met Tad's stare. "I need to shower and get to the salon. I can't... I need a... I need to process."

DOUG DIDN'T REMEMBER showering, getting dressed, or going to the salon. He was on autopilot, his mind still trying to understand what he now knew and saw. It had only been a couple of hours and every part of Doug realized what Tad told him was crazy. Still, all of it, real. He'd seen it with his own eyes. So, now what? Did this mean all those psycho religious nuts were right? He swept up his station, not even remembering who he'd just worked on.

No.

Tad was one of the sweetest, most tolerant, nonjudgmental people around. Even back in New York, after the thing at the club, Tad hadn't pressed charges. He had let the incident drop. Still, Doug and Minx insisted Tad take those self-defense classes so nothing like that could happen again. At least it was their hope.

He's never hurt anyone.

If Tad's an angel, then there must be a God, which means heaven and possibly hell. Which means religion was right, but who was right? How did it work? What do the angels do, and how are things managed? And if there are angels, then there are demons, right? What about them? Did they really all fight? No. That couldn't be it. It's too much. And what about...? Doug steadied himself.

Tim. Shannon.

"Are you all right?" Eddie asked.

Doug jumped, almost dropping the broom.

"Sorry." Eddie walked over and leaned against the wall of Doug's station. His thin frame was hidden by the baggy clothes he was wearing. The pants barely staying above his hips. "Are you sick or something? You look awful, and you've been sweeping the same spot for, like, ten minutes."

Doug shook his head. "I'm fine. I just didn't sleep well."

"Too much partying?" Eddie teased and pointed to Doug's belly. "You need to take it easy, Doug, and that's saying something, coming from me."

"Don't I wish."

Eddie's gaze narrowed as his brows raised. "Have you responded to the invite yet?" He rolled up the sleeves of his shirt.

"What?"

"Mayoral Candidate Hernandez's campaign sent you an invite. Her office has called twice already." Eddie lowered his voice and leaned in. Doug got a whiff of his sweet beachy cologne. "How much have you given her campaign, anyway?"

"It doesn't matter."

Eddie frowned. "What do you mean *it doesn't matter*? You've been all over this election. What is it about her you like so much?"

What is Eddie going on about? I can't deal with this right now. What am I doing here?

The door to the shop dinged, and Eddie peeked out at who entered. "Your husband's here."

"My what?" Doug said, confused and not sure where to look at the moment.

"Tad." Eddie pulled himself off the wall, tugging up his pants but not enough to cover his black and blue boxers. "I need to get things set up for your next appointment. So, you kind of need to move." He reached for the broom.

Doug nodded and handed it to Eddie. He rubbed his sweaty hands on his pants and walked over to Tad.

"Hi." Tad waved, a big bright smile on his face.

"Hey. Tad," Eddie called. "Looking good, man." He went back to cleaning up Doug's station, pulling out fresh towels, and checking the supplies.

Doug turned to Tad. He was dressed in jeans and a green shirt. It made his eyes pop. In fact, the outfit made everything pop. That's why Doug had bought it for him at Christmas a year ago. The man could wear anything and look amazing. No wonder he was a flipping angel. This was insane—he shouldn't be ogling an angel. Well, a former angel.

Oh God, I'm so screwed.

"What are you doing here?" Doug asked in a hushed voice as he pulled Tad past all the stylist stations and into the back of the shop where they had a little privacy.

"I always work on Thursday."

"But you're...well... I mean, I can't have you washing towels and doing inventory." Doug raked a hand through his flat hair. "It doesn't seem right. You shouldn't even be here. Shouldn't you be feeding the poor and sheltering the homeless?"

"Doug, I do my volunteer work on Friday and Saturday. Don't you remember?"

Doug rubbed his face. He hadn't shaved today, and he hated the messy feeling. Still he was impressed he was even up and functioning, given the bombshell Tad had dropped on him last night and this morning. This was nuts. "But you...laundry... I can't..."

"How else am I supposed to make money? I want to get my green card, and I'm gonna need money to do it. Plus, I have—"

"Tad! Enough!" Doug shouted. He froze and glanced over his shoulder at Eddie. He hadn't noticed, thank God— *Wait. Could he do that? Should he say that? Was it blasphemy?* He lowered his voice. "What does an angel need with stuff?"

"Former angel." Tad's shoulders dropped. "I'm human now."

"Hardly." Doug remembered the knife sticking out of Tad's chest. Not to mention how good-looking he was. No human could possibly be as handsome. Okay, that wasn't true...or was it? "Why are you here?"

"I'm being punished."

"Well, not anymore," a deep male voice said.

Doug jumped. He and Tad faced a blond man sitting on the counter. The man wore black slacks and a light-blue dress shirt with the cuffs rolled up. He had blue eyes and chiseled features. Doug gasped at how beautiful the man was. He made Tad look ugly and dumpy.

"Who... What... How..." He was unable to put his words together.

"Fate?" Tad dropped to one knee. He rested his arm on it, his head bowed.

"Tad?" Doug glanced between Tad and this man. He looked over to Eddie to see if he saw any of this, but Eddie was frozen in place with the broom in his hand. Out the front window, nothing moved. People were frozen there too. The cars had stopped, and Doug was shocked at a bird stuck in place just above a parking meter. Everything was still. The world was silent.

"What's happening?" The room spun and things grew dark.

"Not today, big boy," a woman's voice said from behind Doug as a groggy darkness overtook him. Doug's head pounded. A pair of arms grasped him, and someone tapped Doug's forehead. "There ya go. No more fainting for you, and your headache, hangover, should be gone too. You're welcome."

Doug's head stopped pounding, cleared of the fog and darkness. He was alert and his heart rate was back to normal. The colors of the world were more vivid than anything he could remember. Even the smells only slightly tickled his nose; nothing was overpowering. Every scent was fresh and wonderfully fragrant. Like the air after it's rained.

Doug turned to face the woman. She had long black hair and high cheekbones. Her almond-shaped brown eyes seemed to smile at him. She was gorgeous. "I've been keeping my eyes on you, Doug."

"Tad." Doug's voice shook. He waved his hand near Tad's shoulder but missed it.

Tad peeked up at Doug. "That's Death."

"Oh, God." Doug wanted to sit or lean on the counter, but his feet weren't working or listening to his brain's commands. How was any of this possible? "I need... I need... I... Oh, God... I mean... Oh, hell..."

"Doug, breathe," Fate said, his blond hair hardly moving as he spoke, his gaze fixed on Doug. There was warmth and kindness there, giving a feeling of total and complete peace. Doug could have stared at those eyes for eternity. They were heaven. He was sure of it.

"I need for you to take a deep breath."

Doug nodded, then fanned his face.

I have three angels in my shop, and the world is frozen. How can I be tripping when I didn't take anything last night? Is this what it's like to be sober?

"I, um. Wait, there is more than one Angel of Death? How many are there? Oh, God... I mean..."

"Of course there's more than one Angel of Death," Death said, her gaze as bright as her smile. "No way one of us could do it all alone. Given how much you like to kill each other, there would be a line of souls for millennia if there was only one of us."

Doug tried to nod.

Fate slid off the counter. "Stand up, Death. No need for formality today." His voice boomed, bouncing off the walls, but it wasn't loud or angry. Fate's voice was bigger than the four walls of Doug's shop, probably bigger than the building. Heck, bigger than the whole of San Jose. His voice should have hurt Doug's ears, but it didn't.

Tad stood but kept his head bowed. "I didn't think I would see either of you again."

"Well, like I said, your punishment is over." Fate's deep voice rattled the mirrors. His slacks and shirt pulled perfectly at his body, not a wrinkle to be found.

"But I..."

"No buts." Fate rested a hand on Tad's shoulder. "We're here to take you home. Return you to your work."

Doug turned to Tad, still trying to focus on his breathing. "Tad, what's happening?"

Tad raised his head and licked his lips. "This is Fate. He's an Archangel, and she's another Angel of Death."

Fate bowed his head in Doug's direction.

The female Angel of Death winked at Doug.

"You're both so beautiful." Doug instantly regretted his words—*idiot*. "I mean. I'm sorry." He bowed his head.

Should I bow? Should I kneel like Tad did? Should I even be talking to them?

Fate walked over and lifted Doug's chin. "It is both our blessing and our curse. We have seen what happened to Death moments ago in New York. You have no reason to apologize. You are only human. As Death has—"

"Tad, I go by Tad now," Tad interrupted.

"Very well." Fate offered a slight bow and his golden locks of hair brushed past his shoulders. "As to our appearance, it is for aesthetic reasons, nothing more. We find humans react better to us when we take on a perfect form. Would you prefer this aesthetic?" Fate waved his hands over his body, and his appearance shifted.

The man's honey-blond hair grew pale and his crystal-blue eyes turned dull and milky. His strong chiseled features softened. His shoulders went from broad and strong to sloped and weak. He hunched forward and his clear angelic complexion became pockmarked and red.

"I didn't realize we could change our appearance." Tad's eyes grew large, and a smile crept over his face.

"Only Archangels can," Fate said, his voice gravelly and weak.

"I don't understand." Doug blinked several times, taking in the sight of the man now in front of him. Tad had always said the physical was just aesthetic, and what mattered was on the inside. How was this even possible? Then why pick an attractive form? Why not be short and dumpy all the time? Was it like Fate said? We were easier to deal with? Maybe some of the angels were plain. Maybe that is how they move among us.

How many angels have I passed? How many have I not even known were angels?

Fate waved his hands, and he returned to his angelic appearance.

"Must you show off, brother?" The female Angel of Death shook her head, staring at her fingernails. She even yawned.

"Why are you here?" Doug asked. What could they possibly want with him? Sure, coming to see Tad made sense, but why wasn't he frozen like Eddie and the rest of the world?

"Well, the car accident yesterday set in motion today's events." Fate stepped to Tad, addressing him and not Doug. "It caused a minor ripple, one we will correct soon enough. Still, you exposed yourself to Doug."

"In more ways than one," the female Angel of Death said, with a playful wink at Doug.

Doug wanted to throw up. Had they seen them together all those years ago?

Oh God. How was I supposed to know he was an Angel of Death? He was just a hot guy.

Neither Tad nor Fate responded to her comment, which Doug was thankful for.

"I didn't know what to do." Tad gnawed his lower lip. "I didn't realize I was only going to be punished for five years. I... Doug... He's been my friend and I..."

"You foolish child," Fate chided, with a trace of amusement, running a hand along the side of Tad's face. "Five years is nothing, and you exposed a human to the truth because you didn't know what to do." He shook his head. "I thought I trained you better." Fate wagged a finger at Tad. "I gave you too much leeway." A slight frown crossed his lips. "My gentle hand with you has always been your problem, Death. You don't think. You act. Why do you think I punished you?"

Tad gazed at the floor.

For the first time, Doug saw hints of red on Tad's neck. Was he embarrassed, or was he angry? Doug wasn't sure.

"September 11, 2001 was but one small incident." Fate sighed. "October 17, 1989—you are so proud of your work. I had to go and rewrite fifty-four thousand lives because of you."

Tad's shoulders dropped, and tears spilled to the tile floor.

"September 21, 2051—your favorite time—you think you got away with so much, but I protected you. Always cleaning up after your mistakes..."

"Hey now." Doug stepped forward. "Be nice. Tad cares about us. He helps people. No one is kinder and sweeter than Tad."

"All angels are kind and sweet," Fate said. "After September 11, 2001, I needed to make a point."

"You made your point." Doug's neck grew warm. "When I found him, he was barely alive, living on the street. He was starving. Eating who knows what. Living like an animal. No one should have to live that way."

"Yet you have no problem allowing people to live in those conditions now. How many people have you helped, other than Tad?" The Angel of Death narrowed her eyes on Doug.

"That's not fair. I do help, maybe not has much as I should, but the need is great and I'm only one person."

Fate raised a hand and turned to Doug. "He was being punished."

"For saving people." Doug found his voice. No one was going to treat Tad this way, not with all the good he had done. Angel or not, Tad was more of a saint than anyone. "You punished him for saving people. Ridiculous. Why did people have to die? Why did any of it have to happen? If more of you helped us, maybe we wouldn't be in the trouble we're in." His hands balled into a fist. "If you angels cared more, like Tad, maybe Tim wouldn't have overdosed. Maybe, Shannon would still be alive!"

Fate tilted his head to the side, and he glanced over at the female Angel of Death.

She nodded. "I don't know about a Tim, but Shannon Drew Anderson, born 1980 in Clearwater, New York. He was an abused soul." Her voice grew soft. "He left this world before his time. I took him to his destination."

Doug faltered and reached for the chair, then collapsed down with a thud. His heart pounded and tears danced around his eyes. "You took Shannon?" His voice was weak. "Please, is he all right?" He faced the female Angel of Death and wiped at his eyes.

"I cannot say," she said. "I only move the souls on to where they must go." She stepped forward and rested a hand on Doug's shoulder. "Do not mourn for him. Even though I can't say where he is, I know he is free from pain."

Tears dropped from Doug's eyes, and he nodded, taking a shaky breath.

My God. How can I move forward, knowing all this?

Fate crossed to Tad. "Your punishment is over. It's time for you to come home."

"What about Doug?" Tad kneeled before him and held his hands. "I can't leave him, not like this. Please, don't be cruel, Fate. Give him peace."

"As you wish, I will alter these last two days so this reality will forget your indiscretion. I will replace those events with mundane events. I know you share a connection with Doug. I wanted to allow you this moment, but seeing the pain this encounter has caused your friend, I realize it was a mistake." Fate shook his shoulders and his wings stretched out. "Take my hand, Death. It's time to come home."

Chapter Six

"DEATH, IT'S TIME," Fate said again, holding out his hand.

"I can't." Tad stared at Fate's offered hand but didn't take it. How could he? He had too many questions. The possibility of him being human—well, almost human—for five years had emboldened him to question things.

Or, perhaps I've always been this way.

He took in Doug's large form. Fate was asking him to leave his friend, to go back to a job he didn't want. He wanted to stay here with Doug. To be his friend. To share this world with him. There was so much to do and see. How could he go back now? Not like this. Not this way. Doug didn't deserve it and neither did he.

"No." Doug inhaled a shaky breath. "You need to go. You're too good for this world. Always have been."

Had Doug seen the hesitation on his face, or had he sensed it? Tad wasn't sure. "What about you?"

Doug sat on the salon chair. His hair was flat and his eyes red from crying. His unshaven face and bags under his eyes made Doug look tired and beaten. There was no twinkle of life around him today. Still, he appeared every bit the gentle giant he was.

I can't leave my friend like this. What kind of angel would that make me?

"I can assure you, Death, I will take care of Doug's memories." Fate moved forward, his hand still out.

Doug leaned in and kissed Tad on the cheek. "Go on. I have clients and I have stuff to do. I'm sure keeping the world frozen in time, or whatever, isn't good for anyone. Plus, you understand what happens to me when Eddie is holding the broom like that." He pointed and raised his eyebrows several times. "Poor little straight boy. Hmm, might be fun to take off all his clothes before he gets woken up, just to mess with his skinny ass."

Tad shook his head. How could Doug make jokes right now? "Please don't."

"Taddy, I can't... You know how I feel about you." Doug ran a hand across his eyes. "Just, go, please. Fate can do what he needs, and I'll be fine."

Tad stood and glanced at Fate's hand. "Can we talk?"

Fate nodded.

"Oh, wha—"

Doug froze like Eddie and the other humans around him and outside. Only the three angels were active now.

Tad rubbed his chin, a sigh escaping his lips. "What will happen to Doug?" He faced the female Angel of Death. "You said you've been watching him."

Fate nodded to her.

"In four months, I will come to take Doug," she said. "He will be in a car accident and die alone."

Tears fell from Tad's eyes. "No. He can't be alone. Not him, it's not fair. He deserves better. He deserves love and romance."

"It has been written and must happen," Fate said. "Not every life is meant for a happy end. It is how they learn and grow. Heartache and suffering make them human. That is why we came for you today. Once you broke the veil, we could not risk the future."

"Because Doug learned about angels?" Tad's voice cracked. His stomach clenched with both anger and sorrow. This was all his fault. He should have never said anything to Doug last night. He should have known better. Fate was right. He didn't always think, but what choice did he have? Tad glanced around the room. How could he fix this? He needed to help his friend.

"No," female Death said. "It has nothing to do with that. It's his time."

"No! You're doing this to punish me. Because you're afraid Doug will what? Will create a religious faith? That's ridiculous."

"Ridiculous or not, it is still possible, it has happened in the humans' past," Fate said. "However, that is not why we came."

"Then why?"

Both Fate and Death remained quiet.

"If I stay, will Doug live?" Tad's gaze bounced between the two of them. "If I give him the love he wants, the love he deserves, will he be happy? Will his life be full?"

Fate met Death's gaze and nodded.

"What aren't you telling me?" Tad demanded, stepping forward. This wasn't a random person. This was his friend. His only friend. Someone who took him in and helped him. Someone who loved him. He had to know. "If I stay, will Doug live or die?"

"There is more to the answer," Fate said. Several strands of hair dipped over his shoulder. "There are ramifications and events must happen. Doug's life has been written."

"No," Tad yelled. "Then rewrite it. One life, Doug's life, can't be that important to you, Fate. He's nobody, like all those I have saved in the past. You say you had to clean up after me, and that may be, but you cannot allow Doug to die alone with no one in his life. He deserves to be happy. He deserves love and companionship."

"You cannot provide him the kind of love and physical companionship he desires. You've learned this. Come, Death, don't make this harder than it has to be. You have been punished. Don't make it worse." Fate rolled his shoulders back and his wings vanished.

"I can try. He is my friend, and I can't leave him alone. I can't." Tad adjusted his shirt and stood taller. "I *will* try. I will give him all he needs. This body pleases him. He has enjoyed what it has to offer in the past, and he will again. He will have a long happy life if you allow it. If you allow my sacrifice."

"It's not your place," Fate said. "Have you learned nothing these last five years?"

"I've learned to care for these humans. To care for him." Tad pointed to Doug. "They are wonderful creatures, and the Boss was wise to create them the way he did. Despite all their shortcomings, they are good, and they only want love and acceptance. I can give Doug that."

Fate's eyes narrowed. He moved to Doug and ran a gentle hand down the side of his face. He turned to Tad. "Very well." Fate closed his eyes.

"Fate?" Female Death took a step forward. She glanced between Tad and Doug, her expression a mix of worry and frustration. "You can't."

Fate leveled his gaze at her, and she bowed her head.

"Thank you," Tad said. "Thank you, brother. Thank you, sister. You'll see. I'll make him happy. Doug will live a long life. You'll see."

Fate placed his hand on Tad's shoulder. "I'll alter these two days. Once we are gone, your course will be set." Sadness flashed through his eyes and Tad's heart sank. The sorrow from his brother filled his whole body for a moment but quickly vanished.

"Thank you, Fate." Tad inhaled, pushing the sadness out of his memory. He would be everything Doug needed.

A warm white light filled the shop, and when it vanished, the angels were gone. Tad exhaled.

"What the heck?" Doug dabbed his eyes. "Why am I crying?"

Tad pulled Doug to his feet. "Because you love me and I love you." He leaned in and crushed his lips to Doug's. Doug's unshaven face tickled the skin around Tad's mouth as it opened. Their tongues danced.

There was no spark of desire. No stirring of what was in his pants, but it didn't matter. He was going to prove his brother and sister wrong. He was going to make Doug happy. He was going to keep Doug safe. He wasn't going to allow Doug to die. Not today. Not four months from now. Not for a very long time, and if it meant giving Doug the kind of physical pleasure he needed, then Tad would do it. He would never deny Doug, and Doug would be happy.

Doug pulled away. "Tad, what the hell?" He pushed Tad off him. "Just 'cause you almost got hit by a car yesterday, don't go all crazy. You certainly don't love me, and as sexy as you are, we're better off friends." Doug smiled and patted Tad's cheek. "Plus, I'm more woman than you can handle and more man than you can ever get." He laughed.

Doug peered around, his lips pinched together and his eyes narrowed.

"But this is what you want." Tad frowned. "Since we lived in New York, this is all you've ever wanted, and I want to give it to you. I get it now. We can be together. There is nothing stopping us."

Doug raised his eyebrows and waved his finger. "Ah...no."

I was sure this is what he wanted.

"Really? Get a room, you two." Eddie leaned the broom against the wall. "So, what do you want me to tell Candidate Hernandez's people? Or does this mean we get to close the shop early and go see her at the rally?"

"Eddie, how are you ever going to make it in this business if you keep wanting me to close the shop early?"

Eddie laughed. "You wait and see, I'm gonna run this place someday."

"Whatever." Doug shook his head. "You keep telling yourself that. Now go and get my station ready. I'll call Candidate Victoria's office later today. It's kind of exciting. San Jose is going to have its first female Hispanic mayor." He pointed his finger at Eddie to emphasize his remarks. "A strong woman, who is all about human rights and isn't afraid to speak her mind when it comes to idiots like Kim Jong-il in North Korea and those monsters in Iran and the Middle East. I know she can't affect change as a mayor, but who knows where she'll end up." He turned to Tad. "Baby, you okay?"

"I... I don't..." Tad took a step back. His heart was light, but he still hurt. Was this Fate playing a trick on him? Was this more punishment? His face was warm, and the room seemed to spin. He reached for the counter as he tried to understand what was happening. He'd offered himself to Doug, and he didn't want him. But Doug teased him all the time, and sometimes he playfully touched him in ways that would suggest he wanted him. What was going on?

"You know what? How about after my last client today, we go to dinner?" Doug turned to Eddie. "See if you can get us a table at La Fondue tonight. It's short notice, but you tell Jack he owes me a favor for saving him from his awful dye job."

Eddie frowned. "With my help."

"Yes, yes. With your help." Doug pointed to the phone. "Now be a good little intern and go. Shoo." He waved him off, then inhaled. "Okay, Taddy, you gonna stand there and let the towels wash themselves?"

Tad returned to the back of the shop where the washer and dryer waited. He was sure there would be a huge stack of linens for him to clean today. He met Doug's gaze again. There was nothing there. No sadness. No confusion. Just Doug. The same Doug he always saw...well, until last night.

I don't understand. What did Fate do? Was I wrong?

"Tad, honey. Come on. I get I'm an amazing kisser, but snap out of it." Doug caught his reflection in the mirror. "Holy crap. Eddie!"

"What?"

"Why didn't you tell me my hair looks like shit? I need to fix this ASAP." Doug ran a hand through it, making a face at the mirror. "Do I still have razors at my station? I need to shave too. Ugh. I look awful."

Tad's body was a statue. Nothing happened with Doug last night and this morning remained. Fate had rewritten reality, but he still had his memories. *Why?*

"Taddy. Towels." Doug pointed.

"Um, okay."

"Now what was I coming back here for?" Doug shook his head. "Oh, we got the shipment of product yesterday, so if you could take care of it too?" He walked to the mirror. "Eddie, I need product stat. Eddie, get over here." He snapped his fingers.

Tad shook off all his sadness and pain and made his way to the back of the shop.

At least Doug's gonna live, and that's what matters.

THE LAST WEEK had been a haze for Tad. He had tried to talk Doug into a relationship. He even attempted to sneak into Doug's room and give him pleasure, but the more he forced things, the more Doug pushed him away. Saying it wasn't what he wanted and he needed to knock it off. But he had to try, didn't he? He didn't want Doug to be alone. He wanted Doug to be loved and shown love, and he could love him. He was willing, and isn't that what was important?

Clearly, Doug didn't think so.

Finally, Tad stopped and struggled to get back to normal, but part of him still worried Doug wasn't being honest. Now Mike was here—well, Minx because he still used drag name most of the time—and the more time that passed, Tad was running out of options, if any still remained. Minx and Tad had spent hours talking and messaging on the internet, so if anyone could help, it would be Minx. At least he hoped. Tad never talked to Minx about this because of the newness; still, perhaps he could help Tad remind Doug of how he felt about Tad.

"Oh, Minx, honey, you need to move out here," Doug said as they sat at their window table at the Capital Club. "I mean, check out these views."

Tad peeked out the window. Their dinner had been planned so Minx could watch the sunset and see the city lights from the top of Knight Ridder building in downtown San Jose. The building had one of the best views in the city, and Doug had told Tad he really wanted Minx to like San Jose so maybe he would move out here. But Tad didn't think anything would get Minx to move this way, even if Tad really wished he would. Minx loved New York too much.

Minx laughed. "Please, the views are a million times better in Manhattan, and you know it."

"But at least here we get to enjoy them. In New York, it would cost a fortune to have a view like this, and last I checked, neither of us had that kind of money. You remember that dumpy apartment I had." Doug took a deep swallow of wine.

Minx shrugged. "Maybe, but my apartment in Harlem isn't bad, and all my friends are there and so is my family."

Doug finished his wine and nodded.

Minx smiled over at Tad, scanning him up and down. "Tad, you've been really quiet. What's been happening with you? We haven't chatted online in a couple of weeks. Everything okay?"

Tad picked up his glass of water and nodded.

How do I even start?

Doug put down his fork. "Oh, for the love of all that's holy." He leaned in. "Last week, Tad professed his undying love for me and tried to kiss me. Well, he didn't try. We actually did kiss. Then the next night, he came to my room, naked, and tried to..." He waggled his eyebrows.

"Oh my." Minx nibbled at his lips.

Tad's head dropped.

"It wasn't too bad, but we had to lay a few ground rules." Doug leaned back in his chair.

Why did he have to say that? It makes me sound foolish.

Minx laughed. "Is that all?" He patted Tad's hand. "Honey, I've known you forever, and you're one of my closest friends. But you and Doug? Please, we had bets about the two of you years ago, but even we gave up on that horse. You're so much better off as friends." He leaned back in his chair and glanced out the window. "That's the new city hall building, right?" He pointed.

How could he make them understand?

"Yep," Doug said. "Nice. Right?"

Minx shrugged. "This city needs more high-rises. It's so flat. Kind of boring. It's less like a city and more like a giant suburb."

"Hey now. This place is amazing. It's not nearly as crowded as New York. The people are nicer, and it doesn't have a funky human smell that seems to permeate every part of New York...well, especially where I lived."

Tad found his voice and finally spoke up. "But he likes me."

Both Doug and Minx peered over at him, confused.

"I know he enjoys sex with me." Tad was flustered with this whole thing. Ever since Fate and the Angel of Death were here, nothing was the same. And it wasn't like he could say anything. He didn't want to risk Doug dying or something even worse happening. And even a good friend like Minx wouldn't believe Tad's story.

"Tad." Minx squirmed in his seat, then leaned in. He smiled softly.

Doug took Tad's hand. "Like I told you, that was years ago. Tad, honey, we're just friends, and you need to understand and accept our relationship for what it is. It's never going to happen." Doug lowered his voice. "Granted, you are beautiful. Those eyes. Wow. And I'll admit you have several other impressive attributes."

"I'll drink to that." Minx raised a glass.

"You're not helping." Doug glared at Minx, who winked. "But there is more to a relationship. Plus, I know you're not really into the physical stuff, and that isn't fair to me or you. I don't want you to have to force it. And I want to be with someone who doesn't have to pretend to be into me."

"But I'm not pretending." Tad leaned in and took Doug's hand. "I really do care for you."

"I know you do." Doug smiled. "But we're better off friends. Like you and Minx. Or Minx and me. We're good friends. We'll always be there for each other." Doug patted Tad's hand. "I don't want anything to ruin what we have." He touched Tad's cheek. "Do you understand?"

Tad sighed and nodded. He didn't really understand, but he didn't have a choice. Like Doug taught him years back: if someone wasn't into you, you just had to move on. Tad wouldn't move on, but he wouldn't push Doug anymore. He couldn't. No meant no.

The waiter came by and filled Doug's wineglass along with bringing a Coke for Minx and another water for Tad.

"Are all your dinners like this?" Minx glanced back out the window.

"Be nice, Minx," Doug chided.

"Tad, baby, I'm sorry." Minx grinned. "I know what it's like to pine for someone, never to have them return the feelings. I think we all do. It's part of life. A sucky part, but still a part of it. I promise you'll be fine." He leaned in. "And really you can do so much better than this messy queen sitting there."

"Bitch."

"Who you calling bitch? Bitch."

Tad couldn't help chuckling. Seeing Minx here, in person was the best. The whole gang was back together. He really missed this.

"You two need to be nice." A warm smile spread across his face. He hadn't smiled in what felt like years.

"Yes, Taddy," Minx said. "So, tell me all about this mayor person you've been all hot and bothered over. I can't believe my little Dougy is all about the politics these days."

"Oh, Minx, Candidate Hernandez is amazing. She really understands people. Her parents were immigrants to the US and to San Jose." Doug sipped his refreshed wine. "And her mother survived being in one of those South American sex-slave trades, you know real human trafficking stuff."

"No shit!"

"Amazing, right? She really understands human trafficking and human rights. She's very smart, a total friend to the LGBTQ community, and graduated from Santa Clara University. She's just amazing. I'm so excited for her to become mayor."

"You hope," Minx said.

Doug nodded.

"Doug had a fundraiser for her here," Tad said. "He rented out the whole place." He pointed to the dining room.

"Seriously?"

Doug waved it off with a motion of his hand. "Not the whole place, just the banquet hall. It wasn't a big deal. I just made a few calls and paid for the space and the food. I figured I had this membership, so I wanted to put it to good use, plus the house is a little small for an event of that nature. So, it worked."

"Well, I can't wait to see what happens." Minx finished the last of his meal. "What's this place offer in the way of dessert?" He peered out the picture window to the foothills in the east, with all the lights blinking. "I'll admit I'm kind of getting used this view."

Doug tapped Tad's leg and smiled.

Tad's grin deepened. "I like the chocolate lava cake." He was still upset about what happened with Doug, but having Doug as a friend would be good, and he wouldn't have to worry about all the messy sexy stuff. So, it wouldn't be all bad, and as long as they were friends, Doug wouldn't be alone. If only Minx would move out here, then the three of them would be together always.

Chapter Seven

"I'M STILL IN shock." Doug took another hit of his joint. The scent and the flavor filled him with joy after each puff. His fingers tingled as all his body parts started to relax, all his worries followed the smoke trail flowing toward his closed window. This was what he needed. He pulled out his blue dress for tonight's performance. He was prepared with two songs, "Big Girls Don't Cry" and "Bubbly."

"I don't understand the big deal." Tad waved the smoke away. He picked up the black wig Doug pointed to and grabbed Doug's shoes. He waved his hand again at the smoke.

He's always so dramatic. It's only smoke.

Doug pursed his lips, walked to the bedroom window, and opened it. "Because I gave Victoria's campaign a lot of money, and I love what she stands for. I don't think it's right someone as powerful as her got beat out by dumbass Ted Cunningham. Just what we need: another straight white man as mayor."

"But you're white." Tad's eyes narrowed and his head tilted slightly.

"Seriously, how can someone so pretty be so clueless? Tad, honey, Victoria has represented Willow Glen and the rest of our district for two terms now. This was it for her." Doug took another hit. "Mayor or...well, I'm not sure what. I guess she'll go back to being an immigration lawyer. Anyway, it's annoying she didn't win." He exhaled toward the window.

"Okay."

Doug smiled at him. "I know politics is a bummer for you, not being able to vote and all, but who knows, maybe that'll change." He snubbed the tip of the joint with his fingers and then dropped it in the ashtray for later.

A nice treat to help me fall asleep tonight.

"I wish you wouldn't smoke pot."

"Tad, lay off." Doug's voice sounded louder and sharper. "You're not my mother. You know it helps me relax before I perform. Don't kill my buzz." He checked the room. "Do we have everything? I don't want to be late. Oh, and remind me in the morning to call Minx."

"Okay."

"We should stop for Taco Bell." Doug looked around the room. "Crap. Do we have everything?"

"You already asked me. I think so." Tad headed to the door.

"Good, let's go. I want to get there and have a few drinks in me. Loosen up."

Tad scowled.

"What's with you? Since our talk about your declaration of love for me and even after our great visit with Minx, you've been really bitchy. I would have thought your attitude would have gotten better. It's been months." He laughed. "Would it help if I gave you a good fuck again since you seem to be pouting so much?"

"Hey! Not nice." Tad's gaze dropped to the floor.

"You need to try some of my special brownies, get that perpetual stick out your ass."

Tad said nothing as he fidgeted with his wallet and walked out.

Great. It's gonna be one of those nights. Tad really needs to get fucked.

THE MUSIC IN the club bounced off the walls, and Doug felt great. Tonight had been perfect and he had killed his drag. His black wig was teased up perfect and reached for the sky. The blue dress showed off all his curves and made his tits perky and full. Plus there was this hot little Latino boy who kept making eyes at him, and he was beautiful— tanned skin, deep brown eyes, and tall. He needed to keep an eye out for that guy. *Nothing wrong with a guy who likes someone with a little meat on his bones, especially someone hot like him.*

At the table, he swayed his hips in time with the music, checking out the boy again. Doug smiled, mixed his drink with his straw, and took a deep swallow, finishing it off. He frowned down at the empty glass, then peeked up at where the hot guy had watched him. He had vanished in the sea of bodies.

Ah, dammit.

Doug glanced around and found Tad two tables away, talking with Jane Lick, otherwise known as Paul from his salon, and Paul's husband, Denis. They were an annoyingly cute couple who complemented each other. Paul was wacky and fun while Denis was quiet and thoughtful. Doug would have hated them if he didn't know them. There was nothing more annoying than seeing a happy couple, especially when he had no one special in his life.

Someday, I'll have a relationship like theirs.

"Tad, honey." Doug waved and held up his drink. "Go buy Mommy another Long Island." His voice was high and loud enough to get a few reactions from others standing around.

Stare all you want, bitches.

Tad shook his head and crossed over to where Doug stood. "I'm not getting you any more to drink, and please don't shout."

"What?" Doug huffed. Was it the room or him moving? *Who cares?* "I've only had two drinks, and I'm not shouting." He draped an arm around Tad's shoulder. "Come on, baby, get me another drink. I'm sorry about what I said at home. I was just nervous. You know how I get before I perform." Doug smiled and started to whisper, "Tell you what, buy me another drink, and tonight, if you want, and only if you want, we can fool around. Just as friends. I think you might need it. I think you're finally hitting puberty." Doug laughed.

"Don't say that. Please," Tad said and removed Doug's hand, which was lazily creeping down Tad's back.

"You've got such a great body, Tad. Really, it's astonishing you're still single." Doug tried to give Tad's butt a little squeeze, but Tad was too fast. He caught Doug's hand and put it back on the table. "You're no fun. Come on. One more drink and I'll stop."

"I don't want you to drink any more. I'm worried about you, and you have to drive."

"I'm fine." Doug spun around on his heel and wobbled slightly but didn't need any help. "Don't be a buzzkill. I've still got to perform 'Bubbly.' Then I won't drink any more. I swear." He held up four fingers, then lowered one so he had three fingers up, giving a Boy Scout oath. "Water the rest of the night."

"How about a Sprite?" Tad offered and glanced over to the bar. "Or cranberry juice?"

"Screw you. You're no fun." Doug pushed away from Tad. "And to think I was going to offer to bob on that luscious knob of yours tonight." Doug bounced his head to the music as he made his way to the bar. He stopped when a hand held his arm. He glared at the hand and followed it up to Tad's gloomy face. "What the hell?"

"Please, Doug, no more. I'm really worried about you, especially today." Tad didn't move.

"Let go." Doug pushed off Tad's grip. "You're really starting to piss me off. I'm an adult, and I can drink as much or as little as I want."

"Hey, girl." Jane Lick tossed her blonde long-haired wig over her shoulder. "Why don't we leave the boys and go touch up our faces for our next set?" Jane smiled. "I'm a mess, and I was hoping you could give me a hand with my wig. You're hair is amazing tonight. Is that two wigs? Girl, you are a genius. Anyway, I'm just not happy with how mine is laying."

"You, too, Paul?" Doug adjusted the creases in his dress. "Look, I'm fine. I want to have a good time."

Jane glanced at Denis and then over at Tad. "Girl, no one's stopping you from having a good time. Maybe pace yourself with the drinks. Honey, you do not want to fall off the stage. Trust. That shit is nasty, and you look too fabulous."

"Oh, fuck! Look, I'm a big girl, and I can handle my alcohol." Doug's voice was level, and he made sure not to make a scene—or too much of a scene. There was nothing worse than two queens getting into it. "Fine." Doug put his empty glass on the table next to him. "I'm outta here."

"Miss Enshannon, please." Tad's eyes were big like a puppy's, and he chewed at his lower lip.

So fucking cute, but it's not gonna work tonight.

Doug reached into his purse and pulled out his car keys. "Take 'em. I'm getting a cab. Ms. Lick, bring my shit to the shop tomorrow, will ya? Thanks."

Doug made his way through the crowd, not turning back. This was stupid. He wasn't some dumb-ass club kid. He knew how to party and when enough was enough. They were going to be here at least three more hours, and that would be plenty of time to sober up, and if not, they could walk over and get a late-night snack. *Nachos sound really good.* Anyway, he was going to find his hot guy, get a cab for the two of them, and fuck the hell out of him. Maybe two or three times if the vibe was right. He pushed the frown from his lips. He didn't need this shit. Not from Tad or Paul.

It might be time for Tad to move out. Especially since he's clearly not over me yet.

Doug danced his way to the front of the bar. Maybe his hands were accidentally touching a few of the cuter guys as he passed, but he was careful to not cross the line and get in trouble. As he moved through the crowd, he didn't see tonight's entertainment.

"Well, hell," he grumbled under his breath.

He reached the front of the bar, giving the room another peek over his shoulder. On one of the sofas was his soon-to-be Latin lover.

"Bingo." Doug put on his best face and made his way over to him. "Aren't you sexy as hell?"

The guy laughed, tickling Doug in all the right places.

"Thanks." He checked Doug out. "I'm Roberto." He offered his hand.

"Well, it's your lucky night, Roberto. I'm Miss Enshannon."

"I liked your performance and your dancing onstage. Not easy in those shoes." He pointed to Doug's heels.

"Why, thank you." Doug peeked down at his heels and lifted one off the ground. He pulled up his gown to show off some leg—oh yeah, the guy was into him. "These old things? They're just my running-around pumps; you know, housework and dusting. If you want to see something higher, well, you'll just have to come back to my place."

Roberto nodded and lightly licked his lips. "Sure, but won't your boyfriend mind?" He pointed over Doug's shoulder.

Doug turned to see Tad standing over by the bar with Jane and Denis. Tad didn't seem happy, but fuck him.

Doug chuckled. "He's not my boyfriend, just a friend, and not a very good friend lately." He pointed. "And the queen next to him is my sister and her husband."

"Lucky me." Roberto's smile grew. He had an olive complexion and two of the brownest eyes Doug had ever seen. "Why don't we get out of here? I know a great place to get a coffee."

I sure as hell hope coffee is a euphemism for sex.

"Sure thing, cutie." Doug tapped his nose with his finger. "I'm all yours."

Doug offered Roberto his arm, and the two made their way out of the club. Doug didn't bother looking back. Paul would cover his next performance, and Paul and Denis would give Tad a ride home, and in the morning, he and Tad were going to have a long talk.

"DOUGLAS PORTER," A rough voice said, coming from every direction. Every letter like a garbage disposal going off in Doug's head. As far as ways to wake up, this was one of the worst. Was this how Roger sounded last night?

Wait. Where am I?

Doug tried to move. His head instantly pounded, and every muscle in his body was on fire.

What the hell.

He attempted to move again. "Oh God, I'm gonna barf." Doug's eyes flew open. He turned to the side and threw up all over a guy in a suit. The man winced but was unable to move back in time. He stood there as last night's dinner and all the drinks emptied onto him.

"I'm sorry," Doug finally groaned.

I wanna die.

"Ah, hell," the man said. "Thuy, handle this. I got to find a wet towel. Or something to clean this mess up."

"The doctor warned you that might happen," another man said. Was it this Thuy person? He sounded farther away. "Mr. Porter, do you need me to call the nurse?" the calmer, more sensitive voice said.

"What?" Doug considered the space. He wasn't at home or in a motel room with Roger. Wait. Was it Roger? No, Roberto. Crap, he should have remembered. Okay, he might have partied too much last night. But where was he? He tried to focus on the voice and his location. He was in a hospital bed, hooked up to a bunch of machines. He tried to find the location of the voice.

"You go get cleaned up," the hot Asian guy in a dark suit said. He had high cheekbones and a booming chest with a tiny waist. "I'll take care of this."

If I didn't feel like shit, he would be my new favorite flavor.

"What happened?" Doug asked.

"I'm Detective Thuy Tran, and my partner Eric McKee. We have some questions about last night. What do you remember?"

Doug leaned back in the bed, trying to rest his head, but his head was already on a pillow. There were a million pins poking into the back of his skull. How could he remember anything? He took a breath. He remembered the bar. There was a great crowd. He looked amazing, of course. He remembered Tad and Jane giving him shit for drinking. Then he found Roger. No, it was definitely Roberto. He couldn't remember much more. The night was fuzzy. He left the bar with the hot Latin guy. They made their way to Roberto's car and headed back for his place. There was another car...

An accident.

"There was an accident," Doug finally said. "What about Roger?"

Detective Tran shook his head. "The driver, Roberto Mora, is all right. However, the people in the other car weren't so lucky." Detective Tran adjusted his stance and pulled out a notepad and pen. "Do you remember seeing Mr. Mora taking any drugs or drinking?"

Doug shook his head.

"What can you tell me about after you left the bar with Mr. Mora?"

"No, he was totally sober," Doug said. "I remember 'cause he commented on not liking to drink when he drove to the club. I laughed 'cause how do you have a good time without drinking or..." Doug stopped and cleared his throat, but the action caused more pins to gab at his skull. Also, he was talking to a cop and didn't want to say any more.

"So, Mr. Mora was sober, as far as you recall."

"Yes."

"He didn't take anything once he was in the car?"

"No. Well, I don't think so." Doug tried to remember. "No, he didn't. We talked for a bit, then made out. I might have gotten a little handsy, but he didn't say no. We were having a good time. I swear. That's why I offered to go to my place. You know."

"And your home is where you were heading?"

"I... I...think so. He mentioned coffee. I think. I mean we were going to my place. I had partied a little too much, I guess, which is why I wasn't driving. I'm not in trouble, am I?"

The detective made some notes.

"Where's Tad? Where's Jane...I mean Paul?"

"You can see your friends shortly. I just want to get the rest of your statement. It's common procedure in accidents resulting in a death."

"Oh, fuck!" Doug's stomach flipped again. Was he gonna be sick for a second time? "But you said Roberto was alive." He glanced down at the blankets and all the tubes in his arm. The smell of antiseptic and bleach filled his nose.

I hate hospitals.

"What happened to my clothes? I must look like a mess," Doug said, trying to find something to see his reflection.

"You look fine, Mr. Porter," the detective said. "I'm sure the medical staff have your personal effects."

"Can I ask what happened?"

Detective Tran glanced up from his notes. "From what we have gathered so far, the vehicle with Mayor Cunningham crossed the center divide and hit the car you were in. It's a good thing you weren't driving, Mr. Porter. You could have been in some serious trouble. Your blood-alcohol level was through the roof, not to mention what else the doctors found in your blood," the detective said.

"I can't believe this." Doug ran a hand over his forehead, finding his wig was gone. He winced, his head pounding.

"I have all I need for now." Detective Tran closed his notepad. "Mr. Porter, I'm leaving you my card." He placed it on the rolling table thing next to the bed. "We'll be in touch. Once you're out of the hospital, we'll need a full statement."

Doug nodded.

The detective left his room. He was sure the detective had an amazing ass, but he was too shaken to appreciate it. The door had barely closed before Tad and Paul rushed in.

"Oh shit. Are you all right?" Paul ran to the side of the bed and then stepped back. "Gross."

"I...what happened...? I'm so confused." Doug's voice was shaky and gravelly. "Can I get some water or something? My mouth tastes like shit."

Paul grabbed a cup and filled it with water.

"The accident was bad." Tad frowned in a thin line. He had puffy bags under his eyes. "But you're okay, and that's all that matters."

Paul handed him the water. "Oh, Doug, man, I don't know how you managed it, but you are lucky. The news showed both cars. It could have been you and Roberto who died, not the mayor and his driver."

"But how? Roberto wasn't drinking, was he?"

Tad shook his head.

"They tested him before they released him from the hospital. He's fine." Paul sat at the foot of the bed.

"I'm so glad you weren't driving." Tad rubbed Doug's arm. "Doug, I don't know what I would do without you. I'm so glad you're all right. It could have been you. They told me it was supposed to be you, but you're going to be okay."

Poor thing, he's terrified, but so am I. We're allowed to not make any sense right now.

Doug met Tad's gaze. "I'm sorry. I won't ever do that to you guys again, especially you, Taddy. You— I could have died. Oh, fuck. I got to get my shit together. I guess I owe fate, don't I?"

Tad frowned and turned away from Doug.

Paul smiled. "You have one hell of a guardian angel watching after you."

Doug nodded and took Tad's hand. "I'm so sorry."

DOUG TOOK A deep breath, walked into the office building, and made his way up the stairs to the landing. It had been six months since the car wreck with Roberto, and they had quite possibly been six of the worst months of his life. He'd had to deal with the police investigation and then with the media and the public reaction from the death of Mayor Cunningham. The only good thing to come out of the whole thing was Victoria Hernandez becoming the mayor of San Jose in a special election. Unquestionably a shitty way to become mayor, but she won, which was pretty exciting.

I should go. I don't need to be here. No. I promised Tad.

He reached the second floor and walked to reception. This was one of the crappiest receptionist areas he had ever seen. The furniture looked like something out of a bus station, and the desk had fake wood laminate that was broken and peeling off.

What can you expect in a nonprofit? It would be weird to see a plush lobby with the latest decorations.

"May I help you?" a pretty Hispanic woman said from behind the desk.

Doug peered around the lobby. Other than it being ugly, it was empty, which was good. Of course the office was empty. It was six o'clock, and still he didn't want to be here. "I'm here for the group meeting."

"Go ahead and sign in." The receptionist pointed to the clipboard and then handed him a guest badge. "The meeting is down the hall; at the end there, turn right. The door should be open. Okay?"

Here goes.

Doug nodded, clipped the badge to his shirt, and ambled down the hall, passing pictures of staff who had been with the agency for five, ten, fifteen, twenty, and thirty years.

"Wow!" He turned right at the end of the hall and strolled through another door that was propped open. A set of double doors greeted him, and he stopped to take another breath. "I can do this." He straightened his shoulders and pulled down on his shirt, making sure it wasn't sticking to his stomach. "Relax."

Everything makes me look fat. I should go home and change. I can come back next week.

He shook his head and stepped through the doors. There were ten people milling about the room, chatting. Doug took in the sight of the conference room. For everything the lobby wasn't, this was even less. *This place needs a makeover.* An older woman walked up to greet him.

"You must be Doug." She offered him her hand. "I'm Dr. Mickle."

"Hello." Doug checked the conference room. There was a mix of people here from all walks of life. His heart pounded in his chest, and beads of sweat dripped down the sides of his face.

She smiled at him. "Relax. There's nothing to worry about. The first meeting is difficult for everyone." She pointed to the chairs in the circle. "Why don't you find a seat? We'll be starting in a few minutes."

Doug took a shaky breath.

I don't want to end up like Tim. I don't want to end up dead and alone. I have to do this. Not for anyone else, but for me.

His head pounded with each beat of his heart.

I can do this.

Chapter Eight

BEFORE RUSHING AROUND the kitchen, Tad stopped to check the lasagna in the oven. The mixed scents of basil, rosemary, garlic, and olive oil filled the area. He took a deep breath and beamed. He eyed the loaf of French bread as a bark sounded.

He peeked down at Snoopy. "Well, stay out of my way."

Snoopy's nub tail wagged as she backed off, giving Tad room, but she was close enough to pounce on any scraps that managed to find the floor.

Tad grinned and grabbed the bread to cut it up.

Everything has to be perfect.

The buzzer on the lower oven signaled the heat was to temperature. He quickly cut the bread and poured the butter and garlic on top, adding a nice drizzle of extra virgin olive oil. He loved the buttery garlic aroma. Once ready, he put it in the oven to bake. Snoopy barked again, and Tad scratched her head.

It only took Doug two years to agree to let me get you, so don't ruin this.

He met Snoopy's brown-eyed gaze and gestured to the living room. Off she went. Her wagging nub shook her entire backside. The dog was a beautiful black-and-brown cocker spaniel mix. Her health now was better than when they'd rescued her from the animal shelter. The vet hadn't been sure she would survive, but Tad had known better.

Tad was connected to her at once, and he'd known she would have a wonderful long life with them. Animals always loved and obeyed him, which hadn't changed since becoming human.

"Okay, now where was I?" Tad inhaled and glanced around the room. The table was set with fancy white china and crystal glasses. He'd even managed to iron the tablecloth, which was a lot harder than he'd thought it would be. The kitchen countertops were cleaned and polished. The food was almost cooked. The final touch were the fresh linens on Doug's bed and lighted candles so the bedroom and the back of the house had a warm welcoming scent of sandalwood. "Five years." He crossed his arms over his chest, and a familiar warmth rushed through him. He was happy. He was content, but mostly he was at peace.

After Minx's visit, which had become a yearly event, especially after Minx heard about Doug's car wreck, Tad realized his friendship with Doug was all Tad needed to be happy. Fate and the Angel of Death had kept their word, which pleased Tad. Doug was doing great. The salon was a huge success, and Doug had given up drinking and pot. Everything was perfect, and Tad couldn't be happier. His iPhone alarm went off, and he pulled out the lasagna. He checked the bread, then peeked over his shoulder as the door opened.

Perfect.

"Oh my God, Tad, did you see the news?"

"No. What?"

"Mayor Hernandez is going to run for the open California senate seat. Isn't that amazing? I knew it. I knew it all along. I swear she is on track to become not only the first female president but also the first Hispanic president. Won't that be great?" Doug hung his jacket on the coatrack.

"Ah, very good." Tad shrugged. He didn't see why that mattered so much. It wasn't like these people actually did anything. Well, at least as far as he could tell. They sure talked a lot and said they were working hard, but Tad wasn't so sure. There were homeless all over the place, and people didn't have enough to eat, even here in San Jose. And there was violence that Tad flat-out didn't understand.

Doug hurried over and dropped his backpack on the chair. "It's so cool. The shop was all abuzz about it." He stopped and sniffed the air. "Wow. Someone's been cooking."

Snoopy rushed over and jumped at Doug's leg, her non-tail wagging.

"Ah, there's my good girl." Doug knelt and rubbed the cocker spaniel's head and then scratched her back. She flopped to the ground and rolled over so Doug could rub her belly.

Tad leaned against the counter and watched the two of them. For a man who didn't like pets, Doug sure loved Snoopy. He loved seeing Doug so happy. Since he'd gotten sober, he was a lot better off and seemed more at peace. Not to mention he had actually lost some weight, not as much as he wanted to, but some. Overall, he just came across as healthier and nicer to be around.

"So, what's the special occasion?" Doug stood and walked to Tad. He took a deep breath, a smile crossing his lips. "Did you get your paperwork? Has your citizenship come through?"

Tad's smile slipped momentarily. It stung because he still didn't have his citizenship. The immigration counselor told him it would take a while and was a long process, especially with the odd circumstances of Tad's case. Still, three years seemed like a long time to wait.

"No, not yet."

"Well, crap." Doug took Tad's arm. "It's not my birthday, thank Christ. I don't think I'm ready for thirty. Oh, I know, RuPaul called and personally invited me to be on Drag Race? I knew it. I'm gonna show those bitches how it's done. 'Cause you know... I am the next Drag Superstar." He struck his classic pose of his right leg outstretched, resting on his toes. His left hand raised and pointed to the ceiling, glancing over his right shoulder and blowing Tad a kiss.

Tad laughed.

"So, no to RuPaul. Bummer." Doug let out an overexaggerated sigh as he relaxed his stance. "Oh, well. Her loss."

Tad grinned. "You and Roberto. It's been five years."

"Oh, right," Doug said, and his smile turned into a sad frown. His gaze dropped to the floor.

"What?" Tad ran a hand over his buzzed hair, his heart skipping a beat. "What is it? I thought Roberto made you happy?" Tad looked over his shoulder at the kitchen. Everything was set and perfect. He even made those fancy individual chocolate brownie desserts Roberto liked.

Doug poked Tad in the stomach. "Gotcha."

Tad crossed his arms over his chest.

Doug poked Tad's belly again. "Hmm, looks like someone needs to hit the gym. I don't feel perfect six-pack in there anymore."

"You jerk." Tad batted away Doug's hand.

Doug giggled and stepped back.

"You had me worried. I went through all this trouble and you were messing with me."

"Oh, lighten up. I had to tease you. I can't believe you did all this for us. Did I ever tell you how much Shannon loved to cook?"

Tad shook his head.

"No. I suppose not." Doug glanced out the dining room window and sighed. He turned and faced Tad, then sashayed into the kitchen. "What do you need help with?" He fluttered to the sink and washed his hands.

"You can do the salad while I finish the bread." Tad made his way to the oven and checked the bread. The top was just starting to sizzle and it had hints of brown. He smelled the tantalizing aromas and licked his lips.

A few more minutes and it'll be ready.

"You know, it's not just Rob and I celebrating."

Tad glanced over his shoulder. "What?"

"You and me. We've known each other for ten years. Can you believe it?" Doug pulled out the salad. He checked the knife, studying it for a moment. A frown crossed his lips but was quickly gone. He started cutting up the radishes. "We've been through a lot, you and me."

Tad nodded.

"I owe you so much, you know." Doug put the knife down.

"You don't owe me anything. You saved me. I'm the one who owes you." Tad opened the oven and pulled out the garlic bread, then placed it on the counter.

"Fine, then we saved each other." Doug went back to his chopping.

Snoopy barked and jumped at the front door as the latch clicked.

Roberto peeked in. "Hey there, Snoop." He gently pushed the dog out of the way and came in. Tad glanced up from the bread as Doug rushed over to the door, greeting Roberto with a hug and kiss. He still lifted Roberto off his feet. It was sweet.

Moments like this were what Tad lived for. Seeing all this happiness and joy. Even if things didn't work out the way he thought they would, they had worked out for the best.

"There's my sexy man," Doug said.

Roberto chuckled, returning Doug's kiss. "Something smells amazing."

Doug put Roberto down.

"Oh, you know me." Doug took his hand and pulled him toward the kitchen. "I just whipped something together."

Roberto laughed.

Doug patted his upper chest.

There was nothing there, but Tad knew he was pretending there were pearls there. Doug had told him the reference was to an old TV show Doug liked.

"You don't believe me. Gasp." He put a hand to his forehead, then laughed.

"How's it going, Tad?" Roberto said through his chuckle, trying to ignore Doug's silliness. "I see you've been cooking."

Roberto was calm and reflective, while Doug was bubbly and full of life. Their personalities complemented each other. Roberto supported Doug's entertaining and even encouraged him to go bigger, but Doug wanted to focus more on his shop and only did drag for fun these days. The two were a match made in heaven. Tad hid his smile at the thought.

Doug pushed Roberto's arm away. "Hey, I helped. I'm working on the salad."

Tad chuckled. "Well, I wanted to do something special for you guys." He glanced at the wall clock and took in one more assessment of all the food he'd made. "Okay, so everything is ready, and it's time for me to vanish and give you guys some alone time."

"What?" Doug said. "You're not staying?"

"Of course, I'm not. I did this for you guys. It's your night, not mine. I'm going to meet Paul and Denis. We're going to check out that new movie *Contagion*. It's got Gwyneth Paltrow and Matt Damon, so it should be good." Tad went to the sink and washed his hands. "Anyway, you have the whole place to yourselves. There are candles lit in the back of the house, in case dessert leads to the bedroom." Tad winked.

"Tad, man, you don't have to do this." Roberto's brown-eyed gaze met Tad's. "This is too much."

"Of course, I do." Tad dried his hands.

Doug being happy and safe with you in his life should be celebrated.

Doug came over to Tad and hugged him. "What would I do without you?"

Tad's phone dinged and he picked it up. "That's Paul." He typed out a text message, walked over to the coatrack, and grabbed his jacket. "Have fun." He leaned down to kiss Snoopy on the head. "You be a good girl. Go to my room and leave Rob and Doug alone."

Snoopy licked his chin and then headed off to the back of the house.

"Someday, you're going to have to teach me that trick." Doug beamed, watching Tad. "Have fun." He waved, giving the house one more glance. Everything was set for them to have a wonderful romantic evening.

"You too." Tad opened the door and made his way to the car with Paul and Denis. He peeked over his shoulder and nodded.

This is how a human life should be.

TAD STOOD IN a large conference room with all the other volunteers. The smell of coffee and perfume filled his senses. This space had all the basics, but nothing was fancy. Functional at best, and right now, everything was pushed against the back wall so everyone could stand and hear what was going on.

He couldn't vote yet, but that didn't mean he couldn't be involved. Doug suggested he spend some time learning about the political process from the inside and see how they can make a difference. So, he decided to work on the campaign for Victoria Hernandez. He was truly enjoying it because today they got to hear from her and meet her.

This is so cool.

"I'm not running for the senate to serve special interests," Victoria said from the front of the room. "I'm running to stop those who would prey on our youngest and most vulnerable. Working here in San Jose as mayor, I've seen the victims of countries with appalling human rights. I've talked to the women and girls who had to cross the border of our great county, using their bodies as currency as their children watched. All to flee violence worse than anything most people could imagine. All in hopes to get here so they could give their children a better life."

This made Tad sick. It reminded him of his own experience. He had been so lucky that day Doug had found him. He had good people looking out for him. Who would look out for all these others?

Victoria Hernandez would.

"As many of you know, my mother was a victim of the sex-slave trade in South America. She was lucky. She got out with the help of my father, but what about those who aren't so lucky? Not just in South America, but in places like the Middle East, North Africa, and Asia. Who will speak for them? If not us, then who? If not now, when?"

There were claps and cheers from the room.

"It's been ten years since 9/11, and our world is no safer. Not for lack of trying or the billions of dollars spent. We have to hold people and countries accountable, both allies and foes. Look at North Korea and its history of human rights violations, not to mention their push for nuclear weapons that will someday be able to reach us—not Washington, DC, but us here on the West Coast. Seattle, Portland, San Francisco, LA, and yes, San Jose. While we're worrying about the countries in the Middle East, no one is paying attention to them." She paused. "Perhaps when Kim Jong-il passes, we'll get lucky and the people of North Korea will demand change, like those in the Middle East during the Arab Spring, but can we afford to wait?"

There were hushed noes from the group.

"What will we tell all those victims of the Asian and South American sex-slave trade and human trafficking? It's not just about fixing the problems here at home, and trust me, I'm not blind to our own issues. As your next senator of this great state of California, we'll address all these concerns. Where California leads, others follow. If we work together, there is nothing we can't accomplish."

There was loud applause and cheers. Tad clapped along with the others.

"Thank you all for giving my campaign your time and your money. You know how hard I worked for San Jose. Once I win in November, the real work in Washington, DC, begins." She smiled and waved to everyone, then moved through the audience, shaking hands, thanking them for all their hard work and support.

Tad waited his turn to greet Ms. Hernandez. Finally, she walked over to him and took his hand. "Thank you for all your hard work and support of my campaign," she said with a bright smile and a firm handshake.

"I'm really happy I can help you. I think you're amazing, and I'm so glad you're going to help all those people. We need more people like you in the world."

"Your words are very kind. Thank you." She moved on to the next person.

Tad backed away. He left the conference room and returned to the phone bank where he was calling people to ensure they got out to vote. His little workspace wasn't much, just a computer with names and numbers for him to call. In front of him was a script to read so he didn't forget what to say. It was easy, and he knew what he did here would help everyone know about Victoria's beneficial work.

Tad had a good feeling about the direction his life was taking, and he couldn't wait for the future.

Chapter Nine

DOUG AND ROBERTO'S bodies moved in time with the thumping music. The atmosphere was alive with positive energy and everyone dancing, talking, and drinking. Excitement filled him and the space. How could it not? Victoria Hernandez had won the seat in the senate. Yes, they were losing a great mayor, but they were gaining an amazing senator. This was the start of something big. As they danced, Doug leaned in and gave Roberto a peck on the cheek. He glanced over to Tad who was actually out on the dance floor having fun—*good for him*. It made his heart swell seeing Tad enjoying himself. He had worked so hard on her campaign.

Of course, Doug had done his part. No fancy fundraiser for her, but still, he made sure he gave her campaign everything he could. He and Tad had put yard signs in their front yard, and Doug had signs all over his salon. He didn't care if some people didn't like it, but most did. He was proud of his support for such a powerful and amazing woman.

"You need to come back and perform," Roberto said as their bodies moved around the dance floor with all the other revelers. "I miss watching you onstage. When you're there, the world stops. All eyes are on you, and it's magical."

"You're so full of it." Doug laughed. His whole body felt light. Everything and everyone was as it should be.

Life was perfect. Sure, he missed performing every week, but who had the time, between the salon and Roberto? Plus, he wasn't twenty-two anymore.

"I'm serious. Everyone misses Miss Enshannon. You need to bring her out." Roberto put his arms on Doug's shoulders as they continued to move. "Especially with as delicious as you look these days."

"Hey." Doug pursed his lips and raised his eyebrows.

"You've always been sexy as hell, you know. Now you look even more sexy," Roberto said and nuzzled Doug's cheek.

"It's hard. I've been so busy with work. Eddie's a full-time stylist now, and I just can't find a good intern." Doug leaned in and rested his forehead to Roberto's, the rest of the room vanishing as they spoke. "I've gone through so many trainees who aren't cutting it." He waggled his eyebrows at the pun. "I don't think I was ever young and immature."

Roberto laughed. "No. Not you, *mi amor*."

Doug chuckled and fanned himself. "I need some air." He pointed to the bar area near the patio.

"Sounds good." Roberto took Doug's hand and led him through the mass of bodies and over to the sitting area. "What do you want to drink?"

"Cranberry fizz."

Roberto winked and walked off.

God in heaven, I love watching that man walk away. His butt. Those legs. Woof.

Doug sat on the barstool at the table he'd commandeered as the music filled every corner of the club. He enjoyed being out now, not having to worry about performing or his dress and wig. *Thank God, no heels.* Still, he should get out there and perform again. A special tribute for Shannon, especially since it had almost been 15 years since he died. *Maybe in the spring.* Paul would let him, now that he had taken over the show from the former host. Doug still couldn't believe the name Paul picked. "Lick'em Till They're Wet." *Ugh.* He laughed. There was nothing he could do about the name, it was Paul's show now. Plus, things changed.

Still, I'm gonna talk to Paul about the name. Especially if I'm gonna perform in it.

"Hey, Doug." Tad plunked down next to him.

"Taddy, honey, you having a good time?"

"It's fun. Everyone is excited and enjoying the party."

"And who was the cute boy you were dancing with?" Doug leaned forward, raising his brows.

God, I hope he finds someone.

"Oh, Jon." Tad glanced back to the dance floor where Jon was still dancing. "He's a guy I got to know while volunteering at the campaign center. He's nice."

"And will we be seeing more of Jon?"

Tad chuckled. "No, it's not romantic. Jon's got a girlfriend. See?" Tad pointed. Jon was now dancing with some pretty little redhead.

"Well, hell." Doug leaned back.

"What?" Tad beamed. "I love seeing people like this. Everyone is in such a good mood. This is how it should be all the time."

Doug laughed and patted Tad's leg. Even after all these years, Tad never lost the innocence about him. Tad had a special kind of magic. It was part of his DNA and reminded him a lot of Shannon. Doug let out a soft sigh.

Fifteen years—has it really been so long ago?

"Well, next year, you'll be able to enjoy the party, now that someone is a citizen." Doug pulled Tad over and kissed his forehead. "Baby, I'm so proud of you."

"I can't believe it." Tad beamed as he inhaled. "I nev—"

Everything around Doug froze. No music. No loud talking. The laughing stopped. Even the smell of beer and sweat vanished. His heart sank. He checked the dance floor and no one moved, not Jon and not his girlfriend.

Was Jon's girlfriend twerking?

Doug pulled himself together and reached for Tad. "No. Not again." He shook Tad on the barstool he occupied next to him. His heart banged in his chest, and his hands trembled. "Wake up. Tad! Wake up!"

"It's been a long time, Doug," Fate's deep voice said. "Well, a long time for you. We just left you moments ago. So, really no time at all."

"Tad! Wake up." He slapped Tad across the face. "I can't do this again. Please. Tad. Wake up!" His heart hammered, and his body ached to run, but he didn't move.

"He can't hear you. No one can," the female Angel of Death said, flicking her hair over her shoulder. She smiled at him.

"Why are you back?" Doug let go of Tad, seeing the two angels turn from the table next to him. "Why am I only remembering you now? What did you do to me?"

"We blocked your memory of us from before." Fate smiled at Doug. He was every bit as beautiful as the last time with blond hair, chiseled features, and broad shoulders. He even had the same clothes. *Don't they own anything else?* "Instead of eliminating it completely, in case we needed to speak to you about Tad."

"It's some of my finer work." The female Angel of Death examined Doug with her beautiful almond-shaped eyes. "You seem happy and well."

"I am. I haven't had a drink in over four years." Doug sat as tall as possible, using all his weight and height for whatever advantage it would give him against two angels. "I'm clean now, thanks to Tad." He stopped and glanced over to Tad, still frozen. "What do you want with him?"

"We need him to come home." Fate's strong voice bounced around the room, filling the quiet. "His punishment is long since over. He is missed by his brothers and sisters."

"Why are you talking to me and not Tad?" Doug fanned his face.

Fate sighed. "Last time he wouldn't leave because of you." Fate spread his wings.

Doug's heart continued pounding, but not as badly as before. He took a breath to prove his lungs still worked. "That's not how I remember it."

What do they really want? I wish Roberto was here.

Doug glanced over at the bar. Roberto stood ready to pick up two drinks. He was frozen in some awful pose that didn't seem natural.

"True, but you didn't hear the full conversation. You must trust us. Tad does not belong here. You know it to be true," Fate said, his blue eyes blazing into Tad.

Doug couldn't believe he was seeing those big white wings again. How had he not remembered their first encounter? Not even in his dreams did he see such beauty and power. He was small and insignificant in their presence and yet they were here to speak to him and needed his help.

No. Something isn't right. They would speak to Tad, not me. I'm sure of it.

"Now you are happy, in a relationship that brings you both physical and emotional joy, so we need you to help us convince Tad it is time to return." Fate pointed over to Roberto. "I hope he pleases you. It wasn't easy to write his life for you to be together. In his original life, he was to be a university teacher in Costa Rica. He was well respected and very happy. He was single then, but he had many friends and a wonderful extended family. I'm glad he is equally as happy here with you."

"You changed Roberto's life to be here? How?"

"It's not hard, but getting the details right takes practice. Sadly, he is only a high school teacher here, but he seems to do well." Fate offered a satisfied nod. His wings billowed in some breeze Doug didn't sense.

"He loves his job as a Spanish teacher at Silver Creek High School. Everyone loves him there." Doug caught sight of the female Angel of Death, moving drinks around and changing how a few people stood. "What's she doing?"

"Her job," Fate said. "She's making small changes to this reality so these people will meet their proper end."

"Tonight?" Doug's stomach dropped to the floor and returned to its starting place.

"No." Fate touched Doug's arm. "Don't worry. It will be some point in the future. The small changes she makes now will set them on the course they are meant to be on."

"Like with Roberto?"

"No." Fate shook his head. "Death wasn't involved. That was all me."

"So, there's no free will. We're puppets and you manipulate us." Doug didn't like what he was hearing. If their lives were already written, then what was the point? Why even exist?

"You always have free will," Fate said, resting his hand on Doug's arm. "You didn't need to go to your first

AA meeting. You could have walked away. Roberto's parents didn't need to move to the United States. They could have stayed in Costa Rica. I would have found another for you. His life sketch matched yours, and so the match made sense, in a way you were meant to be."

"That doesn't sound like free will." Doug frowned, glaring at Fate and moving his arm.

"I'm not explaining it correctly." Fate tugged at the cuffs of his shirt and took several deep breaths. "You have infinite choices and you make them. I work with the choices you make and offer others to deliver you to where you are meant to be, if such interaction is required."

"Not free will." Doug crossed his arms.

Fate sighed. "I suppose not in the way you think, but I assure you I did not manipulate you to put the tattoo on your behind, nor did I have anything to do with you picking out those purple satin boxers you enjoy wearing. I didn't make you go to beauty school, nor was I involved in your choice to remove your parents from your life." Fate's voice was soft and firm at the same time. His frown made Doug's shoulders drop. "I would have altered it if possible. Your parents were not the monsters you believed them to be. They missed you every day and regretted what they did when you were young. I wish you would—"

Doug's face heated. "You don't know anything about them. Or me." He went to stand.

Fate raised a hand. "I do not judge." He lowered his hand. "Please sit."

Doug returned to his stool.

Fate continued, "Your desire to move to California and buy your shop was all yours as was your choice to buy your home, a smart move on your part. I only changed a few things here and there."

Doug's mouth dropped open.

"So, tonight, we show ourselves to you again and wish to enlist your help in bringing Tad home."

"But he's happy."

"Is he?" Fate asked, plunging his hands deep into the pockets of his pants. "When we left, he wanted to make you happy. He offered to be your happiness, and you pushed him away. You did not want him—"

"We're friends. I couldn't do that to him. I was a mess, and I knew it. I couldn't admit it at the time, but I was barely hanging on. If Tad didn't push me, I would've ended up dead in a ditch, alone."

"Yes, you would've." The female Angel of Death returned to Doug and Fate. "I told you I was watching you. I knew where you were heading." Her gaze never left Doug's face.

Doug fell silent.

The night at the bar. The car accident. I felt something. Like I was supposed to die, but I didn't. I lived.

"You lived, and I took two other souls from this world." Death sighed and tossed her long black hair over her shoulder.

"That wasn't my fault. I didn't..." Doug couldn't say any more. Something about this didn't seem right. Why were they telling him all this? What did they really want?

"No." Fate's voice softened. "Not your fault, nor your doing, but regardless, you lived, and two others died. It set you on your present course. My promise to Tad is complete, and now I ask you to help us convince him to come home. It is your turn to save him."

Doug shook his head. "I...something...what aren't you telling me?"

Death's eyes met Fate's. He flapped his wings slightly and took a breath. "This course Tad is on has ramifications, and we must address them. We must fix what is to come. The future, this current course needs to be repaired. We must be able to rewrite the future for all your sakes."

"I don't understand. This doesn't make any sense. You're angels. Can't you just snap your fingers and fix what needs fixing? Why do you need Tad?"

"Tad only remains because of you," the female Angel of Death said. "And as a human, you understand it is not healthy for anyone. You've become his world." She shook her shoulders and her wings appeared.

How they didn't hit anything or knock anyone over was beyond Doug. He inhaled at the beauty of her wings. There seemed to be a warm glow reflected off them, but there was nothing to cause it. How was any of this possible?

"He can no longer be here." Fate touched Doug's shoulder. "His very presence and interactions alter what is to be. We cannot risk the end of creation as we know it."

"So...he's a wild card you can't account for?" Doug ran a sweaty hand through his hair.

The Angel of Death nodded.

"Will you help us?" Fate asked.

Doug stood and walked over to Roberto. He took in the bar. "Why does the weight of the world suddenly feel like it's taken residence on my shoulders?" Doug crossed back over to the angels and glanced down at the table. If he could stop something bad from happening, he should try. "I don't think I have a choice."

Chapter Ten

"I CAN'T BELIEVE it." Tad smiled, a sense of accomplishment filling every part of him. He didn't even mind having to push the few hands he encountered away from his crotch and butt. Of course, dancing with Jon and his girlfriend, Vicky, helped. "I couldn't have done this if it weren't for you."

Doug was no longer sitting next to Tad. He had vanished from the barstool. The club was quiet and Tad turned around. Everyone was frozen in position. All sound and movement disappeared. The stale smell of the bar gone.

"Tad, honey." Doug's voice shook as he rushed over to Tad's side.

Doug's hand rested on his arm. It trembled enough to make Tad's whole arm quiver. He pulled Doug closer to him. Doug was pale and beads of sweat dotted his hairline.

Those bastards.

His neck warmed and his hands balled into fists. "Fate, you promised to leave me and Doug alone."

"I never made such an agreement." Fate's voice boomed but somehow sounded unruffled. Hints of sorrow rang through his words. "Brother, you need to come home. It's time. You can't keep hiding in the human realm. Your presence here—"

"No." Tad's voice rumbled from his chest. "I don't want to return. I'm happy. I fit in." He rubbed Doug's arm and smiled at him.

It'll be all right.

"Are you?" Doug's face was pale and tears danced around the edges of his eyes.

"What did they say to you?" Tad pointed at Fate and Death. "You were not supposed to bother Doug anymore. Even I know interference on this level has unimaginable punishments."

"You know so little, brother," Fate said. "Please do not insult us."

Doug patted Tad's arm. "Oh, baby, they haven't done anything. We just talked. I promise."

Tad's eyes narrowed as he examined the three of them. Why was his brother, his teacher, here again? And why did he bring Death with him? They needed something. Or something was wrong?

"What did they say?" Tad took both of Doug's hands in his as his eyes grew larger, focusing on Doug, blocking out everything else. Doug's hands continued to shake, and his pulse was strong enough to cause his skin to vibrate with each beat. "You can tell me. They cannot harm you. It's forbidden."

"They're worried about you." Doug met Tad's gaze. "They're worried you are affecting the world. But I don't care about that." Doug licked his lips. "I want to know if you're happy. Are you only here because of me?"

"No," Tad said, but his heart got heavy as his gaze dropped. Doug was his friend, and he wanted to make sure he had a happy life. Was he only here for Doug, or was he here because he enjoyed living as a human? They went to eat at all kinds of different places, and he did a lot of volunteer work. He found he loved to cook. He got his citizenship and now could get a regular job, but he still worked at Doug's salon, and he only had a few other friends. "I..."

"Tad." Doug shook his head. "I can't be your world. I can't be why you're here. You have to do what you were meant for. I'm fine. I'm happy. You helped me. I have Roberto, and he's wonderful. Please, don't stay here just because of me. Go and be an Angel of Death; help people like Tim and Shannon. Be there for them."

"But I'm happy." Tad's voice was barely a whisper. He couldn't meet Doug's gaze. Suddenly, the floor was more exciting than anything happening around him.

"Are you, brother?" Fate took a step forward, reminding Tad he was still here. "I've watched you. Everything you do is for this human and his well-being." He lifted Tad's chin and started into his face.

"What's wrong with that?" Tad snapped. Shaking his head free of Fate's hand.

"Because Doug is only one human." Death's voice was hard and tense, but her gaze was kind. "There are many more you could help. You should help."

Death reached for Tad's arm, but he pulled away.

"I got punished for helping, remember? Russia 1917. San Francisco 1989. Mars 2051," Tad countered, his gaze dropping. He turned and pulled at his shirt, then pointed to the location of the burn marks on his back. "You took my wings and left me on the streets of New York."

I can never forget what you did to me for helping.

Fate sighed and closed his eyes. "Yes, you were punished, and maybe I was wrong for doing so, but this world, this reality with you in it is not meant to b—"

"So, fix it. You're an Archangel. A Fate," Tad barked, pointing at him. "You can write the world any way you choose."

"Even I have limits." Fate's voice softened as he glanced around the quiet bar.

"I don't believe you. I've seen your work here on this world and the other worlds I've been to. You can do anything. The Boss gave you all the power to manipulate society and even what life there is. What makes this world so special? What makes Doug and I so special?"

"Other worlds." Doug's gaze bounced between Tad and the two angels.

Tad glanced at Doug. He gave his head a slight shake and then relented and nodded, taking a breath. "Well, I've only been to three, but Fate and the other Fates have manipulated a great deal on those other worlds. The Fates wield a great amount of power."

The color drained from Doug's face. "I...well, that is a lot to take in." He fanned his face and pulled out his shirt to circulate more air around him.

"I suggest you sit." The female Angel of Death helped Doug back to the barstool.

"Thanks." Doug sat and continued to fan himself.

"We are confusing Doug." Fate shuddered his wings, and they vanished.

"You're the ones who brought him into this." Tad patted Doug's shoulder.

"Only to gain his assistance," Death said. "You refused to listen to us."

"Why am I so important?" Tad took a step forward. "I'm one of hundreds of Angels of Death. I'm not special. I'm only a few hundred years old. There are others older and more experienced. Nothing about this makes sense."

Fate shook his head. "You still haven't learned. Every life, even an angel, can have a profound effect on a great many things. There are major convergence points that must be reached intact and unaltered for this world to continue. How close are you willing to take this world and these humans to destruction before you decide to come home and leave this planet for the humans?"

"Tad." Doug licked his lips. "Is this really what's going to happen? Are we going to blow up?"

Tad shook his head. "Of course not." He turned to Fate. "You forget, Fate, I've been to the future. I've seen what happens to these people. They have problems, but they continue on. Not only to their moon and Mars, but to other places in the universe. They have a long future ahead of them."

"You saw the future yet to be." Fate raised his hands, palms up. "Now things are in flux, the other Fates and I are not sure what will happen. Not even the Boss is sure anymore."

"Impossible."

"Not impossible," Death said. "Every time we move to a separate point in time, the future is different, and all of them are—"

"Then make me human." Tad shook his head, not wanting to hear any more. Not wanting Doug to hear more. "Make me a mortal." He pointed to Doug to emphasize his point. "Give me a mortal life. A fully mortal life. Faults and all."

Fate waved a hand, and only Tad, Fate, and Death were in the bar. Everyone vanished and the world grew even quieter than only moments ago. Tad heard the blood in his veins.

"What did you do?" Tad demanded, spinning on his heel. Doug was nowhere to be found. He had never seen or heard the world so quiet.

"I took us out of reality altogether."

"What about Doug?"

"He's fine." Fate took Tad's hand. "Brother, what you ask for... Are you sure it's what you want? You will be human. You will grow old and die. Whatever is to happen, it will be out of my hands once I write your mortality. It may solve the problems we face, but it may not."

"I understand."

Fate huffed and studied Tad. "I don't think you do, but I will grant you this." He nodded. "You will be mortal like any other human. Are you sure this is what you want? You will have all their flaws and all their desires."

"What will happen to Doug?" Tad asked. His heart beat faster. Was he sure this is what he wanted? Would it be worth the price? *Of course, it is worth this sacrifice.* But would he remember anything? Probably not, but did it matter? Despite his anger toward Fate, he trusted him to make sure he and Doug were both taken care of, assuming Fate gave his word.

"Nothing. He will continue on his course. Both of you will. Your human life will be only slightly different from the one you lead now."

"And I won't remember any of this?"

"No," Fate said. "But Death will keep an eye on you." He turned to Death. "You will watch after Tad."

She bowed and her wings dropped to a position of compliance. "Of course. He is still my brother, human or angel. I shall watch his life and not interfere."

"Upon Doug's death, I will come for you to bring you home." Fate's voice was gentle as he touched Tad's cheek. "Your mortal life will be tied to his."

"When Doug's life is over, I'll happily come with you, and I'll do as you instruct. You have my word." A small nagging at the back of Tad's brain called out to him he would need to ensure Doug indeed had a long life and this was no trick on the part of his brother. *No. Fate would not do such a thing. I have to believe in him.* Still, something haunted him. He didn't know what, but he had to take this leap of faith. Tad knelt down on one leg and rested his right arm on his knee. He bowed his head. "Thank you, brother."

TAD TOOK A deep breath and dropped back on the bed. Every part of his body tingled, and he was awash with exhaustion. It had been amazing as usual. He smiled over at Sara and brushed the strands of black hair from her face. Her full ruby lips and her deep mocha skin was flushed with pleasure.

Man, I'm good.

"You were amazing." With a great exhale, Tad shifted onto his side, resting his head on his pillow so he could look at her.

Sara took a breath and smiled. "So were you. This whole night was perfect."

Tad snuggled closer and wrapped an arm around her, enjoying the warmth. As much as he loved sex, he adored the intimacy more—these moments when they were both satisfied and their connection was one. Even with as short a time as it lasted, this moment was the best part. This was what people needed to understand about sex. It wasn't who you slept with but the connections you made and held in the moment. Sex was never about the body but the soul. The emotion. The becoming of one.

"Are you going to stay?" Tad ran a hand down the side of her cheek. Her face was warm and there was a slight shiver as he moved his hand. "I make a mean eggs Benedict."

"You want me to stay?" Sara pulled the blankets tighter around her and nuzzled closer to Tad, her heat joining his.

"If you want. I don't mind. I'm enjoying your company, and I believe you're appreciating mine."

"What about your roommate, Doug?"

Tad laughed. "Don't worry about him. He's over at Roberto's. They're having a sleepover."

There was a yip from the floor.

Tad glanced down at Snoopy lying there. "And Snoopy seems to approve."

"All right." Sara leaned in and kissed Tad softly on the lips as he held her tighter. She took a breath, rested her head back on the pillow, and closed her eyes.

Tad leaned in and kissed her lips again, taking in the scent of strawberries on her skin. He would forever associate strawberries with Sara, just as he associated mulled spice with Vince and vanilla with Angela. Scent was such a powerful key to remembering his former partners. There wasn't a day that went by where some smell didn't remind him of someone wonderful. Someone sharing their body with him. He felt his body stir, but not in a wanting way or a way requiring attention. The semi-arousal was in the form of remembrance for those he'd been with before.

It's magic.

He smiled down at Sara. She was already asleep. He leaned back on his pillow and faced the ceiling. These moments of peace were when he could relax. He didn't know how long he and Sara would be together, but for now, he made her happy, and he was contented. He glanced over at her one more time. He took another breath and closed his eyes. Sleep came to him easily.

Chapter Eleven

DOUG SCROLLED THROUGH the news on his laptop and various headlines caught his eye. "Fifteenth Anniversary of 9/11," "North Korea Defies World Again with Missile Launch," "Turkey Closes Border with Syria and Puts Military on Alert," "China Expels North Korean Diplomat," "Guam's Governor Requests Greater Protection, as Concerns over North Korea Increase." With a frown, he shook his head and switched over to the salon's social media page.

At least, I can control this.

He sent out a few updates on the salon's site and responded to a couple of requests. He flipped over and checked his personal social media page for any news from Minx about his upcoming visit. It would be great to see him again. He just wished Minx and Tad got along better.

Doug sighed.

So much drama, all because Tad is Tad.

He switched back to his work calendar, bypassing all the media updates. He couldn't handle reading any more news. He wanted to be in good spirits for lunch.

He glanced down at his phone. "Ugh." He had time before his lunch and needed to at least pretend to work. He peeked at the salon monitors (a necessity to reflect a turbulent time) noting Ashley was working at his station, readying it with fresh towels and refilling product bottles. Even though he didn't have any more clients until later this afternoon, she liked to have it all set for him. He smiled.

Ashley's good.

He closed the web browser and the social media pages. He needed to get some paperwork finished before lunch.

His phone chirped, and he stood and stretched his back and arms, then checked the salon monitors again. All the stations had clients with stylists working away. Everyone seemed to be enjoying the experience. Having a busy salon with pleased clients was what he liked to see. Happy people were good for his bottom line and good for those he employed. The addition of a full nail service, including foot spa, had been a big success, and having the contract aesthetician brought in even more business. If the shop continued to do well, he would be able to expand to the clothing store next door. Turn his shop into a full-on day spa.

I'm on my way. So long as we don't blow ourselves up.

He pushed the negative thoughts aside and focused on his dreams. He didn't want to admit it, but promoting Eddie to salon manager and head colorist was definitely a smart move. Eddie had a knack for color, and it showed in his work. It freed up Doug to work on the shop as a whole, and that freedom was worth every extra cent he paid Eddie. Of course, he couldn't say anything to Eddie. He would want more money, especially with the baby on the way.

At some point, Doug would open up a second salon in Los Gatos or Los Altos and let Eddie buy into the business, giving him the money he needed to take care of his family, and it would help Doug shoulder the cost.

It'll be amazing.

He turned back to his phone. A reminder popped up on his calendar. He needed to arrange his team to go to HairWorld in a few months. It would be great to catch up with everyone there. It was sad HairWorld was the only time he got to see some of his peers and friends. When Minx arrived, he would check with him, make sure he was going, and maybe they could extend the trip a few days, just the two of them, and catch up.

It'll be a nice break for me as well. I could use it.

Of course, the purpose of HairWorld was for work. Trends were always changing. Keeping he and his stylists up-to-date was key to maintaining his business and taking it to the next level. But there was always time for a good friend and a little fun.

He glanced at the folders on his desk and ran a hand over his chin.

I should look into taking some classes. Especially if I want to get this place to the next level.

Doug checked his phone again, seeing the date. "Crap." He tapped over to the salon's message board and typed a message from the salon. He didn't want 9/11 to go by without saying something. Even if it was rushed. Especially since he had friends back in New York, and he still had awful images of that dreadful day. He doubted he would even recognize Ground Zero anymore.

The world keeps moving forward.

The door chimed and Doug glanced at the security monitors. He broke into a smile.

About time.

Doug waved off the folders on his desk and pocketed his phone, then headed out to the main floor. "I was wondering if you were going to show up."

"Man, like I could miss lunch with you." Tad adjusted the collar of his light-blue dress shirt and gave Doug a kiss on the cheek. "You still look amazing."

Doug chuckled. "Right." He pulled at his long-sleeve purple shirt, making sure it wasn't sticking to any of his less than flattering bits.

"Oh, now stop," Tad said. "Where do you feel like eating?" He pulled out his cell phone and checked for messages.

"I don't know."

"Sure you don't." His gaze stayed on his phone. "Come on. I don't have time for games."

Doug stuck out his tongue. "Fine, how about Aqui's or Willow Street Pizza?"

It's my cheat day, even though this stupid diet doesn't seem to be doing any good. Ugh.

"I can do Willow Street." Tad still stared at his phone.

"Great." Doug glanced over his shoulder. "Paul, I'm heading to lunch. Let Eddie know when he gets here."

Paul waved. "Will do. Hey, Tad."

Tad was swiping at his cell phone but still managed a wave in the general direction of Paul's voice.

Doug sighed. "Tell me you're not gonna be playing on your phone all day."

Tad held up a finger. "Just making plans for tonight."

"Seriously?" Doug rested his hands on his hips. "You're such a whore. When are you going to settle down with someone...anyone? We're not kids anymore." Doug checked his hair in the mirror of his station.

Crap, I can see more gray. I've got to have Eddie fix my color.

"Hey, I haven't found the right person." Tad slipped the iPhone into his pocket. "Not everyone can have a perfect relationship like you and Roberto."

Doug laughed as they headed out of the salon and started walking down Lincoln to Willow Street. He loved the smell of fall in the air. The damp autumn air filled with the scent of fresh fallen leaves. There was nothing like it. "I want to check in Mann's on the way back. They're cleaning my rings."

"All right." Tad eyed the couple from hair to shoes as they passed them.

"What about Cindy?" Doug poked Tad in the side to get his attention.

"What? Oh." Tad shook his head. "Nah, she was fun and all but a little too needy."

"David?"

Tad laughed. "He was nice, but you know, there wasn't a lot of passion. Plus, he got hung up on the whole pansexual thing. Not to mention, he had this obsession with being a top. What a waste of a great ass."

Doug shrugged. "Maybe you need to stop thinking with your friend between your legs."

"Hey." Tad pursed his lips.

"It's true. You totally flaked on me and Minx when we were at HairWorld last year in LA. For a married couple you met at a Peet's."

"Hey, come on, so not cool. They were hot, and Minx hates me."

"No. Minx doesn't hate you."

Tad crossed his arms over his chest. "Really?"

"Okay, maybe a little, but you did break his heart."

"Whatever. So, really what was I going to miss? Minx glaring at me and hardly speaking. No, thanks." Tad shook his head at the idea.

Doug sighed as they walked.

"Anyway, I don't only think with my dick." Tad frowned. "People just get hung up on stupid shit."

"You're right. People are screwed up, especially when it comes to sex," Doug said with a confirmation nod.

"I really don't see the big deal." Tad glanced up and down the street at the traffic. "So I don't get hung up on cock or pussy. Who cares? Big deal. It's about the person, not the body parts."

Doug hit Tad's arm. "Language."

Tad chuckled. "Sorry, Mom."

"What happened to my shy, quiet guy I found almost fifteen years ago at the memorial? You were so upset about the attacks you hardly said a word. I had to drag you to the salon to have Minx fix that awful mop you called a hairstyle."

"Hey, I was still processing." Tad checked in the window, raising a hand to his hair. "Plus, being in college didn't leave me a lot of time to worry about my look. Anyway, the whole attack was a lot to take in. Why do you think I went into counseling to begin with?"

"Because you're a frickin' saint and want to make the rest of us look bad..." Doug smirked. "Or it could be you're trying to counter the fact you're a man-whore."

"Oh, stop. I'm not a man-whore."

Doug chuckled. "Please, I've been to your new apartment. You're such a slut. I'm surprised you don't have a condom machine in the bedroom."

Tad pulled his lips tight into a frown.

"Let me guess your schedule this weekend." Doug raised his hands to the sides of his temples. "Saturday will go something like this. You'll have a coffee date, then a lunch date with someone else, and your main date is dinner. You know, the one you want to sleep with, and depending on how *dessert* goes, you'll let them sleep over and cook them breakfast, either eggs Benedict or pancakes and sausage. Or if it wasn't all that, you'll push them out and set up plans for brunch later in the morning."

"No one likes you anyway." Tad nudged Doug as they continued down the street.

Doug laughed much louder than he intended. He turned to cross the street, and Tad grabbed his arm. "What?"

"Pay attention. You've got to check the traffic. You don't want to get hit, do you?" Tad let go of Doug's arm. As if to emphasize his point, a dark-blue Tesla S zipped by. "I may not always be around to save you."

"Only for the big stuff, though, right?" Doug remembered how Tad was always there for all his crazy. The light changed, and they crossed the street with the other pedestrians.

How did Tad or anyone tolerate me with all the booze and drugs? I don't think I could ever pay him back for saving me.

He shuddered at the memory of the night of the car wreck. The night he met Roberto and swore off alcohol and drugs. That night changed his life, and he was so thankful. The wreck was probably why he and Tad had stayed so close all these years. Even though Tad never settled down. In fact, he seemed to become even more promiscuous over the years.

I guess if you look as good as Tad, you can get away with it, even at our age. I'm so glad there was never anything between us.

"So, what do you think about Hernandez running for reelection?" Tad pulled Doug from his thoughts. He opened the door for the two of them. He held up two fingers to the hostess, and she ushered them to a table.

"Well, she's definitely not afraid to speak her mind, which I like," Doug said. "I can't believe how she keeps pushing the boundaries of her senate seat. But I'm wondering if maybe she needs to soften a little, given how turbulent the world is right now."

"Seriously? She's fighting to protect people, and I love how she's not letting these countries get away with their human rights violations anymore." Tad pulled off his jacket and hung it on the back of his chair. "We've needed this kind of leadership for decades."

Doug dragged out his chair to sit. "True. And she has pissed off that pot-bellied dictator over in North Korea, which I kind of like."

Tad chuckled. "I wish I could have worked on her campaign this time."

"Well, I'm sure you sent in a contribution. Plus, you probably already slept with everyone."

"Hey. Not cool."

"But probably true."

Tad pursed his lips, then raised his menu. "Maybe it's a little true."

Doug checked over the various options, with a laugh. "Thought so." He scanned over the day's specials. "I don't know why I bother reviewing the menu since I'm just going to get the lasagna."

"It's good." Tad glanced at the lighter options. "I'm going for the salad."

"Ugh. Really? Come on, Tad. Live a little. I get to cheat today. Don't make me cheat alone." Doug rested his hands on the table.

"Are you kidding? I'm getting old. I've got to work at keeping my body in shape."

"Shut up." Doug pulled at his shirt again, making sure it wasn't caught on his belly or his man-boobs. "You're an ass."

Tad glanced over at Doug with those green eyes and smiled. "You're as handsome as you were the day I met you. You know it doesn't matter what you look like on the outside. It's all in here." Tad touched Doug's chest, right over his heart. "You're a beautiful person and a remarkable friend. Plus, Roberto loves you just the way you are. His love for you is what matters, not all this stupid window dressing." He waved a hand in front of Doug from his hair over his face and down. Then he leaned back and frowned. "I, however, have to work on keeping myself in shape in hopes of finding someone just as amazing. Because of how shallow people are. It's very disappointing. I really do want to find someone as incredible as you or Roberto and settle down."

"That'll be the day." Doug dropped his napkin on his lap. "I wish you would find someone now." He took a breath. "You know Minx will be out here next week, you could—"

"No," Tad said. "Absolutely not."

"I don't like the idea of you being alone."

Tad took Doug's hand. "I'm not alone. I have you and Roberto, Paul and Denis, Eddie and Danielle, plus the folks at work. Trust me. I'm so far from alone. I'm surprised I have time to even meet people."

"I think you're too picky, maybe even a bit of a snob."

"Me?" Tad brought a hand to his chest.

"You know what I mean." Doug checked out the restaurant. He loved the brickwork and the concrete floors. The wonderful scents of Italian spices and pizza filled his nose and made his mouth water. He browsed the various customers. Was there anyone in here for Tad? Tad probably already scoped out the restaurant, but Doug could give it another once-over. Tad deserved it.

"Honestly, even though it would be nice, I'm not worried about it. I'm just enjoying life. If I'm meant to find someone, I will." Tad took a sip of his water.

"Right." Doug tore a piece of bread in half and then dipped it into the olive oil and balsamic vinegar.

"Have you thought about the online dating sites?"

"I use Tinder, Coffee Meets Bagel, Bumble, and Grindr. What more do you want me to try?"

Doug laughed. "Grindr's not for dating."

Tad waggled his eyebrows. "I know."

The waiter walked over to their table. He was tall and trim with a great smile and perfect teeth. His hair was brown and cut neat. He couldn't have been more than twenty-three, still a baby. "What can I get you guys?"

Tad smiled and winked at Doug. "Oh, I'm sure we can figure something out. I wouldn't mind hearing about the spicy sausage you have to offer."

The waiter cleared his throat. His cheeks got rosy.

Doug rolled his eyes.

Same old Tad.

"IT'S SO GOOD to see you." Doug leaned back in the chair, placing his phone next to his plate. They were enjoying their dinner and drinks in San Pedro Square Market. Well, Minx was having a drink with his burger. Doug was having a ginger ale with his falafel. The place wasn't too busy yet, but once the band started, it would fill up. Especially as more people came in from their day jobs. Doug picked up his falafel, leaned over his plate, and took a bite.

"This place kind of reminds me of back home." Minx put down his beer, taking in the various dining establishments and all the people milling about, eating, drinking, and watching TV.

"Kind of." Doug glanced around. He liked the industrial feel of the place. There were high exposed ceilings and polished concrete floors. It had a loft feel but was built for eating, drinking, and music. The rolling doors could be opened to make for both an indoor and outdoor space. It also allowed for great ventilation when the venue was filled with people. "I was chatting with Paul, you know, Jane Lick, and I was thinking... What if you and I pull out our best drag and perform while you're here? Paul said it was a great idea. He would love to have us."

Minx laughed. "I didn't bring my clothes or my wigs out here with me."

"I have stuff at home. We could get ready at the salon and go from there." Doug grinned. "We could make you fabulous. When was the last time Miss Messy Minx made an appearance?"

Minx took a sip of his beer. A distant expression on his face. "It's been a while."

"Me too," Doug said. "Roberto keeps telling me I need to bring Miss Enshannon out of retirement." He laughed. "And Tad..."

Shit.

Minx's expression changed from a bright smile to a scowl in an instant. "I'm guessing he'll be there?"

"I'm sorry, Minx." Doug leaned back. "Yep, I'm sure Tad'll be there. He loves drag shows, and he always loved our performances. You know him."

"Oh, too well."

"Look, we don't have to tell him." Doug leaned in. "Heck, he'll probably be out on a date and not able to go."

"So, he's still screwing anything with a hole?"

"That's not fair."

"But accurate, right?"

"It's not like that."

Minx raised his brows.

"Honey. I know he broke your heart, but how long has it been, what, thirteen years now?" Doug scooted his chair closer to Minx.

"You're probably right. I should get over it, but walking in on him with another person..." Minx shook his head.

"I think he was still hurting from the 9/11 attacks. It was a hard time for him."

"Oh, come on, Doug!" Minx frowned. "I get it. He's your friend and he helped you with all your shit, but come on. There's something wrong with Tad. He only thinks of what hole he needs to fill or have filled. You think he's an angel, but he's not, and he's nothing like Shannon."

Doug's heart ached and tears instantly twinkled in his eyes.

Minx didn't mean to hurt me. Take a breath and breathe.

"Shit." Minx reached for Doug's hand. "I'm sorry. I can't imagine how difficult that was for you, your best friend...dying like that." He shook his head. "Fuck. That was a low blow. I shouldn't have said it, but he just... God, Tad still gets under my skin. And it's not like I'm not over him. I am. He's just an asshole, and I found out the hard way."

Doug swiped at his eyes. He met Minx's gaze, recognized the worry in his expression. Doug forced a smile. "I know you didn't mean anything by it, and I know Tad hurt you when he broke up with you."

"Broke up with me." Minx laughed. "He didn't even have the decency to do that. He just stopped calling. Then seeing him at the bar with a total stranger—you remember the one—the blue eyes and all hands. The bartender— Matt, I think—had to almost pull a hose on the two of them. As it was the guy had his hands down Tad's pants giving him a tug." Minx frowned. "Such a jerk."

Doug sighed. "But he's not like that anymore."

"Really?"

"Are you sure this doesn't have to do with him being open to a relationship with anyone?"

"Don't." Minx pointed and shook his head. "I'm sorry I brought up Shannon in the way I did. I know how much he meant to you, but don't say that. I know many pansexual people, and they don't act like him. I hate stereotypes, and you know it. Tad's just a pig."

Doug sighed. "God, I hate this. Two of three people in this world I love the most don't get along. Will you at least consider—"

The monitors around the market all flashed red as did Doug's phone. Doug grabbed his phone as he and Minx checked the screens. The emergency alert system sounded. The news anchor appeared as a hush came over the whole area. The bartender turned up the volume.

"We're getting word from our correspondents in both South Korea and China the Chinese government has now officially closed all its borders with North Korea. Tensions between the onetime allies have been on the rise over the last several months. We are waiting for word from the White House, but we can now confirm all the borders between China and North Korea have been sealed, and the Chinese military are bringing in heavy artillery and tanks."

"Well, this can't be good," Minx whispered to Doug.

"No. No, it can't." Doug closed his eyes and offered a silent prayer to whomever might be listening.

What the hell is wrong with these people?

Chapter Twelve

TAD STEPPED OFF the light-rail train and took in the surroundings as a few people pushed past him. The courthouse was directly ahead of him, a three-story building finished in the 1880s. In fact, he was amazed they were still using it. He was pleased it wasn't abandoned like so many other great old buildings.

We need to do more.

Tad raised his gaze to the sky, taking in the fresh fall air. With the situation getting worse on the Korean Peninsula, these quiet moments were a relief. Tad took another look at the courthouse, then turned to the park. As nice as the old courthouse was, St. James Park was sketchy with all the homeless, but it was midday with plenty of people around and the homeless normally stuck to themselves. Seeing all the homeless was depressing, really. Tad wished he could help them all, but, sadly, not everyone wanted help.

Maybe they could convert some of these old historical buildings into homeless shelters.

He crossed over to a statue of William McKinley and some nearby benches. He found one that wasn't occupied and didn't have the lingering scent of beer and urine.

Why am I here?

He leaned back and glanced up to the sky again, the trees and a few office buildings also filled his vision. Today was a lovely day, and the view was impressive. The scar between his shoulders burned, but that was nothing new, and he had long since grown to ignore the pain. Except for right now, when it was itching.

Why am I thinking about it?

He shuddered.

Tad adjusted his arms, flexing his shoulder blades, as a pug trotted over to sniff at his feet and leg. The dog's caregiver was this sexy white guy in his thirties with a tight blue polo shirt and a shaved head. Tad smiled at him. The man had dark-brown eyes and a closely trimmed beard. Tad petted the pug's head.

Finally, the guy came over and picked up the pug. "Sorry."

Tad shook his head. "No problem. I love dogs. I have one myself."

"What kind?"

"Cocker spaniel."

"Nice. Well, see ya." The smooth-headed guy waved.

I wouldn't mind feeling that beard between my thighs.

A chuckle escaped him as he continued to enjoy the view of the guy and his dog walking away. "Bummer," Tad whispered. The guy didn't even give him a second glance. He rested his arms across the back of the bench and exhaled. He peered back at the sky. There was a tug at the back of his brain.

Something about this feels familiar.

A shadow crossed over Tad and his shoulders tightened. A shudder traveled through his body.

Right on time.

"What?" The random thought caused Tad to scout around the park, seeing all the people rushing about.

Someone is here. Someone is watching me.

He shook his head.

I'm being stupid.

"No, brother, you're not," Fate landed with a heavy thud in front of Tad. His booted feet left an imprint in the crushed gravel. "We're here." He shook his shoulder and his bright white wings vanished. Death landed next to him and did the same, causing her wings to disappear. Fate and Death marched up to him.

The world froze around him. No one moved. Time had stopped. In the sky, a plane hung silent in midair, like a child's model from their bedroom ceiling. Tad's stomach dropped.

"Why are you here?"

"Because this reality continues down the path to destruction," Fate responded. "Nothing we've tried will fix the timeline." He joined Tad on the bench, and the weight of his body made the bench creak. "Brother, even with you as a human and the small changes we've made to allow you to continue on here, it has done nothing. This world is in danger. The future is completely unknown, and its outcome is a worry to us."

"Too much is changing." Death met Tad's gaze with her soft one. "There are too many deaths, and every time we make a change, there are more. This world will soon end."

"Not possible." Tad glanced at the man with the shaved head and the pug.

"Come, walk with us." Fate stood and reached out his hand.

Tad took the offered hand, and they were standing in Doug's salon. Everyone stood around the large TV screen mounted to the wall. The salon itself had been through a major remodel. It was double the size of the salon he'd known.

Some of what used to be Doug's hair station was now a lobby with several couches and a reception station. Behind the counter were floating glass-and-wood shelves filled with lotions and haircare products. And, behind the shelves, small glass tiles in warm browns and soft yellows and oranges had been laid. They offered the wall a unique design and gave the space an elegant shimmer. Diffused lighting and the sounds of water falling filled the area. Past the lobby was a door with a sign reading: *Relaxation Center—Quiet Please*. Over in the old part of the salon were several new stylist stations. Everything had been painted in creams and browns, and the overhead lighting had been replaced with more direct lighting.

"Doug's Salon?" Tad walked over to the counter and ran a hand over the stone countertop. "It's beautiful. I know Doug talked about doing things like this, but that was like a week ago. Now to see his dream come true—this is amazing. I'm so proud of him and impressed. How long has it been?"

"Does it matter?"

Tad tilted his head and crossed his arms, wanting the answer to his question.

Fate nodded. "As you wish, brother. It's been two years from the time you know. Doug will be able to expand his salon and turn it into a full-service spa," Fate said. "It is quite popular."

"Way to go, Doug." Tad nodded, smiling broadly.

This doesn't seem so bad.

"Does he open another salon?"

Fate nodded. "A year later." He pointed to the television. "We are not here to learn about Doug's business. Watch."

The sound kicked on.

"To no one's surprise, the 2020 Bradley-Hernandez ticket has been declared the winner by all the major networks," the male news anchor said. "Victoria Hernandez has not only become the first Latina vice president but also the first female vice president in US history. Hernandez and President-Elect Bradley promise to continue their hard stance on North Korea and the Middle East. Bradley, in his acceptance speech, reminded everyone a nuclear Korean Peninsula and a nuclear Iran were not something his administration would allow. He's applauded the hard line China has taken and its continued border closure with the North. He would be tasking Vice President-Elect Hernandez to work with our friends and allies in Asia and the Middle East to reach a consensus on how to proceed and solve these global issues. He assured his supporters his foreign policy, however tough, would not take away from his push to strengthen the country's universal health care plan as well as other safety net services."

Everyone in the salon was clapping and cheering. Doug and Roberto hugged. Eddie brought over a bottle of champagne with several plastic cups. Paul and Denis helped pass out the cups as Eddie and Danielle poured.

"This is great," Tad said.

Death nodded. "A great many firsts, but keep watching."

Fate waved his hand, and the room changed.

It shifted from night to day, but the day was gray. Tad glanced to the window. Rain bounced off the sidewalks outside the salon. Small groups of people rushed by, holding their jackets and umbrellas tight. Doug, Eddie, Paul, and everyone else in the spa watched the news. Doug turned up the volume.

"President Bradley has announced the harshest sanctions yet against North Korea. As expected, the isolated country has threatened total annihilation of the United States, China, and any other country who threatens their sovereignty," the news anchor said. "Vice President Hernandez has just finished her seven-day trip in Asia meeting with China, Russia, Japan, and South Korea. This trip is a precursor to President Bradley's meeting with the leaders of these countries later this month. The focus of the upcoming meeting is President Bradley's continued push to hold countries accountable for human rights violations and the rights of victims of the sex-slave trade."

"Sounds like someone is finally doing something about them, and they finally got China to back them up. No one's ever been able to do that." Tad bounced his head in agreement with the TV.

"Keep watching, brother." Fate frowned.

On the TV was a clip of President Bradley's address to the country. "Two years ago, when I first met with then-Senator Hernandez, we agreed we would hold countries accountable for their human rights violations and for any attempts at nuclear proliferation. These are not easy choices we make, but as she reminded me, if we don't speak for those who can't, then who will? If we don't act now, then when?"

Tad crossed his arms.

Fate waved his hand again.

The day changed and Tad glanced outside. The street seemed busy and people were rushing by. The sky was bright. From the way people were dressed in shorts and T-shirts, he assumed it was summer.

The TV screen blinked red and white, and everyone in the spa reached for their smartphones as they also blinked and buzzed with emergency alerts. Doug tapped his device, and the TV volume increased. Out on the streets, people stopped and stared at their devices.

The alert cleared and a TV anchor sat at a desk with a dour expression. "At five a.m. local time, just twenty minutes ago, North Korea launched a surprise attack on South Korea, sending a series of Hwasong missiles, a Scud-class missile, to targets in both Seoul and Busan. It is unknown at this time if the missiles were nuclear-tipped. The president has been rushed back to Washington, DC, from his visit in Germany. All military personnel have been activated. We have gotten reports the closed border between China and the North, as well as the demilitarized zone separating the North and the South, have gone dark—"

"What does any of this have to do with me?" Tad asked.

The world around them froze. Fate stepped forward. "It keeps getting worse. The United States Navy was stationed in Busan. They will be forced to respond, but they won't be alone. They will be joined by Japan, Australia, and New Zealand. All four will declare war. China will offer a military alliance with the United States and back the United States in the United Nations. Russia, for its part, will seal their borders with North Korea and offer no support for the country in the United Nations."

"I'm not seeing the problem," Tad said. "North Korea has been responsible for much pain and suffering since the first conflict."

"Victoria Hernandez wasn't meant for this course. She has been the driving force for much of these events.

As senator, she influenced both members in the United States government as well as China. She was in a position then as a representative of one of the wealthiest states and places in the world. Then as vice president, her influence and power continued to grow," Death said. "The night of the car accident, the elected mayor was not supposed to die."

"So, don't have him die." Tad shook his head. "One life doesn't seem like a hard fix."

"I can't." Death shook her head. "I've gone back and altered his course. He ends up dying no matter what I do."

"Fate, you can make changes," Tad said. "If Vice President Hernandez wasn't meant for this course, then give her another path. If the former mayor was meant to live, then keep him alive."

"I've tried as well. His death was a major convergent point for human history. We did not see it; we did not know, as impossible as that may be. His death is a set point. It can't be altered. We didn't know this would be the case. He's not an important historical figure, so there should have been no issue, but we were wrong. Perhaps, in this timeline, should the humans continue, he is in fact important."

"Then what do you think I can do?"

"If we erase you from this reality, I believe it will reset the convergent point, forcing this realty to change, everything will return back to what it should be."

"And Doug will be dead."

"I'm sorry." Death touched Tad's arm.

"No," Tad said. "You made me mortal, you gave me a human life, and we made a deal. When Doug passes, I will return to you. That was our agreement."

"It was." Fate ran a heavy hand through his perfect hair. "But can't you see this will get worse?"

"No worse than any other war." Tad pointed to the TV. "It's no worse than what has been happening in the Middle East with ISIS and Syria. What makes this so special?"

"I don't know." Fate collapsed onto a couch, his left hand massaging his temple.

Tad had never seen Fate appear so defeated. Fate always had answers. He was an Archangel, a Fate. The Boss had created them for this very reason. How was he not able to fix this? Or was it some trick?

No, Fate wouldn't try to trick me? Would he?

"You must have some idea why this is so different."

"I don't know. None of us do, but it's something." Fate rubbed his face. "Maybe it's actually nothing. I don't know. But the Boss has been quiet as well."

"What do you mean *quiet*?" Tad glared at his brother. None of this made sense. The Fates, the Archangels—they had power greater than an Angel of Death. If they were not able to fix this, then who or what would? How could it be? How could they not know about a "convergent point"? Fates were responsible for keeping the course, getting the humans from one convergent point to the next. "No. The Boss wouldn't just vanish," Tad whispered.

"I'm not getting any answers; none of us are." Fate's gaze met Tad's. "I think this has to play out without his involvement."

"The Boss is always involved, even when quiet." Tad ran a hand over his smoothed-down hair.

"Not this time." Fate shook his head. "None of the Archangels can reach him. We believe the gates to the afterlife have been sealed."

"Not possible." Tad laughed in disbelief.

"It's happening." Death crossed to meet Tad at the couch. "We can't say for sure, but the signs are there."

"You've seen this before?"

"Once." Death's shoulders drooped as she glanced between Tad and Fate. "But that was during the great flood, when the boss was angry." She shook her head.

Tad ran a hand over his face. "And you're saying this is the only option? If I come back from being lost out of my proper time, everything will be returned to normal."

"We don't know anything for sure." Fate rubbed his chin.

"So this is a guess?" Tad scowled at both Fate and Death. "One course of action that may not even work?"

They were quiet.

They are hiding something. Or they know more than they are willing to say. Even now. What are they really doing here?

"I'm sorry. I don't know if I trust you."

Fate's eyes grew large and Death made a move for Tad, but Fate grabbed her arm, holding her in place.

"I'm not going to do this for a what-if." Tad stood from the couch. "I've come to enjoy being human. Once my time is over, you have my word, I'll return. Or until you can tell me Doug's death and my no longer being a human will fix things. I'm not willing to risk it. What if it makes everything worse?"

"You're being selfish," Death snapped. She shook her shoulders and her wings opened to their full length. "You're so busy thinking with the toy between your legs that you can't see the greater good."

"Maybe I am. I'm allowed." Tad pointed at them. "I gave up everything. You punished me. You sent me here.

You threw me to this world and to this reality for years. Now because I don't want to return with you, I'm the selfish one. But I can see you're not telling me all you know. Even now."

"We don't know anything for sure. This is all unknown to us." Fate glanced up at him from the couch. "Please, brother, are you doing this to punish me?"

Maybe I am.

Tad worked his jaw. "Aren't I allowed some happiness? I'm enjoying what a human life has to offer. I've hurt no one. I work, I have friends, and I've experienced all forms of love. How are love and sex selfish?"

"Enough." Fate stood. "Tad is correct. As much as I would like him to come home, we made an agreement, and I will honor it."

"You can't." Death gnawed her lower lip. "We have to fix this before it's too late."

Fate shook his head. His normally straight shoulders drooped. "I had hoped you would return with us, set this right. I will have to find another way, assuming there is one."

Tad took Fate's arm. "Brother, I do understand, and I know you want what is best as I do. I can't sacrifice one life, not anymore." He sighed. "There must be another way. You'll find it."

Fate frowned and his gaze fell to the floor. With a final peek at his brother, he waved a hand.

A shadow crossed over Tad, and his shoulders tightened. A shudder traveled through his body.

Right on time.

"What?"

Tad pushed the random odd thought from his mind and scouted around the park, looking for something, but unsure what. There were men and women in suits, a couple jogging. Two women sat together as a little boy bounced up and down on one's lap. He squinted. Someone was here. Someone was watching him. His phone dinged and he jumped.

He pulled out his cell. "Crap, I need to get back to work."

Tad stood and took one more look around the park. Trees, grass, benches, nothing out of the ordinary, and no one paying him any attention. He glanced to the sky and shook his head.

Something doesn't feel right.

Chapter Thirteen

DOUG ADJUSTED HIS leg on the sofa. It had been shaking and bouncing around for the last half hour. He chewed his nails as he watched the television. The news was a mixed bag of both good and bad. The war, if you could call it that, was over, and thank God the casualties on the Allies' side weren't high. But the loss of life in general was devastating. Another blessing was the war stayed limited to Korea. "So stupid. There should have been another way." Snoopy struggled up on the couch and rested her head on his lap.

"Hey, girl." He rubbed her head.

Doug focused back on the TV. "The reconstruction efforts on the Korean Peninsula continue to move gradually," Vice President Hernandez said to the reporter. "However, President Bradley has met with the new president of Korea in Changwon and has promised additional funding and military support." She smiled and then added, "And we're not shouldering the burden alone. The leaders of Japan, China, Australia, and New Zealand have all offered additional aid."

"Given the level of destruction in both the North and the South and with the loss of Seoul and Pyongyang, don't you think the president's timeline for our total withdrawal from Korea is ambitious? Isn't he worried we might face a similar problem as in Afghanistan and Iraq?"

"The two situations are completely different. With regards to Korea, we have the full support of the UN and the Security Council."

"Still, the timeline, according to some experts, is too ambitious."

"I support the president and his timeline," Hernandez said. "What everyone has to understand is there is no magic wand, but the president with the help of our allies has accomplished a great deal. Still, there is much work to do." The smile never left her face.

She had grown even grayer now that the conflict was over. Doug remembered how young she had looked as mayor—*such a long time ago.*

"I'm here to ensure it happens." Hernandez provided a firm nod, ending any additional questions on the subject.

The reporter's gaze narrowed, but she moved on. "And what about the people of North Korea? How are they doing with the sudden changes and seeing the world as it truly is for the first time? We've learned from the BBC in several towns the people have committed suicide in fear of the US, China, and South Korean forces."

Victoria sighed. "We have heard of isolated incidents. However, the people of both North and South Korea are amazing. Those Korean nationals with friends and families in the North have been allowed into several of the former northern communities and have worked to ease the transition. All the effort they have put into their unification is inspiring. It reminds me of when East and West Germany were reunited."

"But East Germany wasn't as isolated and its people as undereducated on the rest of the world. In fact—"

There was a knock at the door. Doug glanced over his shoulder and got up. Snoopy raised her head, her nubby tail wagging.

"Looks like Tad's here." Doug scratched her back, then moved her head off his lap.

She's getting so old, the poor love. But aren't we all?

Doug grinned down at the dog and crossed the living room to the front door. He checked the security monitor, which showed Tad's roguish grin as he stood there. He unlocked the door.

"Hey there." Tad walked in.

"Long time no see." Doug hugged Tad and gave him a peck on the check.

Tad lifted him up and nonchalantly spun him around, kissing Doug's cheek.

"Put me down, ya goof."

Tad smiled and took Doug's hand as they moved to the couch.

Tad had stronger hints of gray in his hair, but he was keeping it short and slicked back so the gray was hardly noticeable. He still had a solid body, but there were definitely wrinkles around his eyes and some minor lines in his forehead.

Damn if he still doesn't look sexy as hell. I hope he finds someone. How much longer is he going to be able to play the field? Forever?

Doug bit back the smile that was forming at his own little joke.

Snoopy woofed at them, her nub still wagging.

"There's my beautiful girl. I miss you so much." Tad knelt and scratched her ears, letting her lick his chin. "I just can't take care of a dog in my new place."

"She misses you." Doug forced what he hoped was a warm grin. He watched the two of them. Memories flooded back of them first getting the dog. How small she was. How sick. Not to mention how excited Tad was. He fussed over her until she was healthy and bouncing around the house, making a mess of everything.

How many shoes got wrecked because of her?

"Who's my little baby?" Tad said.

Snoopy rolled over on her back so he could rub her belly.

Where has all the time gone?

"We both miss you." Doug continued to watch Tad with Snoopy.

"I know. I'm sorry. I've been busy." Tad stood and brushed off his knees. "Where's your hubby?"

Doug laughed. "He's still down in Costa Rica, visiting family. I thought you knew that?"

Tad shook his head. "Sorry, must've slipped my mind."

"I hear getting old will do that." Doug teased and walked to the kitchen.

"You're such a bitch." Tad joined him at the counter. "Why do I tolerate this?"

"Because I'll always be young and beautiful."

"So, forty-one is young and beautiful."

Doug filled two glasses of water and held one out for Tad. He tried to hide his chuckle with a cough. "Now who's the bitch? And I'll always be younger than you."

"Anyway, so what's the plan?" Tad said. "You know it's not every day you celebrate twenty years of friendship." He took the offered glass and walked around the living and dining room. "I miss this place. It's hard to believe I haven't lived here in...God...how many years?"

"How is life at the fancy Parkview Towers downtown?" Doug sipped his water. "You still like it?"

"Oh man, so worth the wait." Tad grinned. "I'm not living on the top, but still, the views are amazing. I'll have you over next time we get together." He sipped his drink. "I'm telling you, Doug, once you see those views, you'll want to sell this place and move in. Hey, maybe we should eat downtown? Or have you already planned something?"

Doug took a sip of his water. "Maybe."

"Bastard, I knew it. Where?"

Doug shrugged.

Tad chuckled. "Man, after all these years of being around each other, you would think I would know better than to ask you where we're eating. You're such a food tease."

"Har-har." Doug finished his water. "You know, I've been thinking a lot about that all day."

"Dinner?"

"No. About us." Doug rolled his glass in between his hands. "If it wasn't for me meeting Tim, I don't think I would have ever run into you. Think about it. I spent the night over at Tim's apartment the night before. So, the morning I met you, I was leaving his place and, of course, running late. If it wasn't for him, we would have never met."

Tad frowned and continued sipping at his drink.

"I know you never liked him, but he got us together."

Tad rolled the glass in his hand.

"What?"

"Nothing."

"You sure?"

"Yep, just a tickle in the back of my brain."

"Anyway, I was going through some of my old drag boxes and dresses, and I found his phone number on my subway ticket. It even has the date, September 4, 2002." Doug put down the glass, pulled out the ticket from his pocket, and held it up. "I can't believe I still have it. Look at this. Like something out of a time machine." He handed it to Tad. "Fate's a funny thing."

Tad put his cup down and took the ticket. His eyes narrowed. "Fate? Of course. Fate."

Doug's brows raised. "You sure you're okay?"

Tad flipped the ticket over in his hands. He shook his head. "Do they even use tickets anymore? Isn't it all an app, like on the high-speed, light-rail, or BART?" Tad turned it over in his hands again, his typical happy expression was gradually replaced by a growing frown, his attention not leaving the ticket.

Doug shrugged. "I know you never liked him, and for good reason, but really, if I hadn't spent the night at his place, I would have never met you at the memorial." Doug reached for the ticket.

"Well, I suppose that's one positive thing that came from him." Tad ignored him and put the ticket in his shirt pocket and crossed his arms over his chest. "Anyway, what's for eats? I know you planned something. You always do."

Doug laughed. "Okay. Guilty as charged. I thought we could try a new steakhouse at the Fairmont. I made—"

The TV buzzed an emergency alert. Tad and Doug turned to the screeching TV.

"What's going on?" Doug asked as his phone buzzed. He pulled it out of his pocket. There was an alert text to check online, TV, or radio for an emergency broadcast. Tad was doing the same thing with his phone.

Both men made their way to the TV. The screen changed and the network news came on. "Breaking news out of Japan, Guam, and China. A rouge faction from the former Democratic People's Republic of Korea has detonated low yield nuclear devices in Tokyo, Guam, and Beijing—"

Outside the house, the old air raid sirens started to blare. The piercing squeal of the sirens made Doug's teeth ache. He'd seen them around his neighborhood, but hadn't thought they worked. A relic from the past, or so he'd thought. Snoopy jumped from the couch and scurried for Doug and Tad, a trail of urine following her as she tried to find safety from the noise.

"Tad, what's going on?" Doug's heart pounded in his chest, sweat beading on his forehead. There was a map up on the TV. Then it flashed to the emergency alert screen again.

This can't be happening. What's going on? Do we run? What do we do? What are we supposed to do?

"I don't know," Tad said over the sirens. He pulled the ticket from his pocket and glanced down at it. "Fate. Why?" The ticket seemed to glow in his hand. Tad closed his fist around the ticket.

"Tad, what's going on?"

They turned to the TV. There was nothing but a red-and-white emergency alert symbol.

"Where's the news?" Doug's voice was frantic. "Are they going to launch more weapons? Are we launching bombs? I thought we had a missile defense thing? We're not doing this. We can't. Roberto!" Doug yelled. "Oh God, what do we do? Tad, what are we supposed to do?"

Outside the house, a crash sounded like two cars running into each other and then the sounds of shouting.

This house doesn't even have a basement. Where do we go? Why isn't the TV broadcasting anything?

He took Tad's arm. He wanted to cry, to find a place to hide. How was this happening? Why was this happening? Why was Tad focusing on his hand? Why wasn't Tad doing anything? Things were supposed to be getting better. Isn't that what they were just saying? The world was supposed to be safer. This couldn't be it.

"It's okay." Tad pulled Doug toward him. Taking his face in his hands. He held Doug's gaze in his own. "It's a test or something. Maybe a warning."

Doug tried to nod. There was another crash from outside, and a car alarm went off. He jumped, but Tad held him so tight. He wanted to believe Tad. With all his heart, he wanted to believe Tad.

This is madness. We were just talking about how well things were going. What are these idiots doing? How can this be happening? They were supposed to be making the world a better place.

The power in the house blinked out, casting them into darkness. "No!" Doug's yelp was cut off by his heart in his throat. The sirens continued to blare outside. Tad lowered his hands and pulled Doug close and tight.

"Stop it," Tad called, a heat radiating from him.

Tad placed a hand on Doug's head and pulled him closer into his chest.

"Who? Who's doing this? Who are you talking to?" Doug spoke through sobs.

"I remember. Just stop it. I know what to do. I know what I have to do."

Chapter Fourteen

TAD STARED OVER Doug's shoulder, glaring at the ticket still in his hand. Why was Fate allowing this to happen? Everything was coming to an end. Every part of him sensed it. The moment he saw the old subway ticket and Doug started talking about Tim. Doug was right. If it wasn't for him meeting Tim, he and Doug would never have met and none of this would be happening.

Tad peeked around the living room. The Deaths were all around them. The nuclear attacks on Tokyo, Guam, and Beijing were pushing the humans too far. There was to be all-out war, and there would be no survivors. There was no backing away from this cliff, not like in October 1962. At least back then, they weren't dealing with madmen. Maybe they were, but not like now. *The road to Hell is paved with good intentions*. The old saying came to mind.

"Enough," he shouted again, his arms still wrapped around Doug. "You've made your point."

Snoopy was at their feet, whimpering. Doug's head was buried in Tad's chest. He could feel the tears through his shirt. Doug held him so tight he was sure he would have bruised ribs.

"I said, enough," Tad yelled, glancing around the dark room and then up at the ceiling. "I know you're here, brother. Enough of this madness. Stop it now!"

Everything froze and Tad was alone. The house was empty and the noise of the sirens stopped. The world was silent; the only sound was the drumming of his heart. The scent of Doug's cologne and the slight ocean-mist smell that always seemed to fill the home with warmth and love had vanished. There was nothing. Just a room filled with things, but no life and no love.

"Why?" Tad asked, wiping the tears from his eyes. "Why did you do this?"

"I had to make sure you were ready." Fate rested a hand on Tad's shoulder. "Your penance has been served."

"You were willing to destroy this world to make a point?" Tad turned to face his brother. He met Fate's kind gaze. Fate's soft lips formed a straight line, his brows and eyes lowered. There was no joy in his expression. There was nothing but sorrow and pain; however, in his eyes, a twinkle of hope appeared.

"No. I needed you to learn the truth." Fate moved to the couch and sat. "I needed you to learn one small change, no matter how insignificant, can make all the difference. What you did on 9/11? Not only were *you* lucky. Very lucky, Death. But I had to manipulate lives to cover for you. This isn't a game. Yes, you made a positive impact on a few lives, but how many others suffered because of your new chain of events? It could have gone badly, like now."

"But it didn't."

"But it could have." Fate's voice raised. "The meeting between Doug and Tim, the slip of paper, a small thing. A single event set these events into motion. One small change in the wrong direction and it could be all over. We do not have the luxury of pushing our morality onto these humans. They do enough of that on their own."

"I only wanted to help, to make up for all the pain I caused when I was...one of them. I hurt so many people back then, Doug and my parents most of all."

"I understand your life ended at a young age." Fate reached out a hand to Tad. "I know you missed out on a lifetime of growth and experience. Clearly, the joys of bonding and closeness were what you missed and needed most. I know this...but...you can't be with Doug right now, not anymore." He placed a hand on Tad's cheek. "You will remember it all."

All the memories of his life as a human rushed back to him. It was like remembering a long-forgotten scene in a favorite movie. Once you remembered, it brought back both the joy and the sorrow.

Tad pushed the memories away for the moment, walked over, and sat. Fate joined him. "Why Doug? Why all this?"

"You know why I picked Doug." Fate's gaze narrowed on him. "You know more than you'll admit, even now, but that's for later." He ran a hand down the side of Tad's face. You have learned a great deal in this short time. You have learned more than some who are three times your age." Fate's voice was soft and the tone was gentle.

Tad pinched at the space between his eyes. "This was cruel."

"Yes." Fate nodded. "I will not deny it. But I took no joy in my actions, and I'm sorry."

Tad browsed around the home he had once known. He remembered the day he and Doug moved in. The night he cooked Doug and Roberto dinner. The day they brought Snoopy home as a sick puppy. The night he became a human and experienced his true first act of lovemaking. Every memory was here from both alternate realities he lived and from his past life. It had all been a test. None of it was real.

Or was it?

"Are you ready to come home?" Fate's crystal blue-eyed stare met Tad's. "Are you ready to fix this world? Are you ready to have your wings returned?"

"I don't know if I'll ever be ready." Tad sighed. All the joy and pain. Even the heartache filled his memories. So many emotions. It didn't matter if they were fully real or not because they were his. They were real to him, and he needed them. He would carry them with him. Always.

Fate smiled. "You finally learned." He stood.

"Was any of it real?" Tad asked.

"All of it."

The heaviness in Tad's heart lessened, and there was peace where only sadness and pain had been. Knowing the realness did more for him than knowing they would be able to repair this world and return all the lives that had been needlessly wasted.

The wall with the now-silent TV centered between two windows dissolved into a sea of bright light. Tad took a final breath, trying to capture one last scent of Doug and this house, his house.

"Take my hand, brother. It's time to set things right."

I STRETCH OUT my wings. It feels good to have them back. They are white and beautiful. The weight is like a long-lost friend who has returned to my life. A joyful burden. I forgot how good they feel. Being back in New York, seeing all these old ghosts is almost too much. But I love humans, and I love this world. I experienced great pain and great happiness. I know what it's like to be human, and I like being Death better. As good as I tried to be as a human, I was selfish and didn't make the kind of difference I can make now. The lesson was difficult, but here is where I belong—*well, for now.*

I'd be lying if I said there weren't parts of my life I missed. Some feelings will never fade; however, I have my memories and that's wonderful. They are mine, and I can revisit them anytime I want without harming anyone.

I cross the street, spotting a pay phone. In 2002 New York City, they're still around, which is lucky for me and the rest of the world as it would turn out.

I like the aesthetic of Tad. It's easy to transition into a busy crowd, especially in a city like New York, where people don't always pay attention. Too busy, I guess. I'll use Tad this time. It helps that I'm in jeans and a button-down shirt that both Doug and Minx would be proud to see me in. I walk to the pay phone, deposit the coins, and dial the number. Of course, I have the number memorized from all my time working there. Even if I didn't, I doubt I would ever not remember it.

"Village Salon, this is Minx. How can I help you?"

"Hello," I say. "I'd like to make an appointment with Doug, please."

"Of course, you one of his regulars?"

"I'm a referral."

"Wonderful, give me just a sec." There is rustling around in the background. "His next appointment is September 8th at two p.m."

"Oh no, that won't work," I say, using my best panicked voice. "I have a hair emergency. I've got this audition tomorrow, and my ex took a clipper to my hair..." I trail off for effect. It's a little lie, but as Death, I'm allowed.

"Well, if it's an emergency, I can take you today."

"You don't understand. This is bad, and I've been told to only trust Doug. Is there anything you can do? I'll pay triple in cash."

"Seriously? Damn, you must be desperate," Minx says. "Tell you what, give me your number, and I'll call you back."

"Can't you check with him now? Please. I'm freaking out. I don't know what I'm going to do. I've got to get this part. I know it's small, but it could be my big ticket." I cringe at my unfortunate joke. "I'll pay four hundred dollars. Please, it's all I have. Who needs food, right? Please, I really need this fixed, and I know Doug can do it. That's what everyone says."

"Okay, hold on," Minx says.

I hear the phone get put down on the desk as Minx calls Doug on his cell.

Doug is supposed to have tomorrow off, and Minx is set to cover for him, but I know Doug needs cash for rent and is only taking the day off to go buy new shoes and a dress for his performance next week. Plus, four hundred dollars is a lot of money, and Doug would never say no. Thank goodness I know Minx well enough to understand he would never steal a client, no matter what.

"Honey, you got yourself Doug. Four hundred dollars for the rush, and he's coming in on his scheduled day off," Minx said on the other end of the line.

"Oh, thank goodness. You guys really are the best. I'm sorry if I was rude," I say. "I just can't believe what Tim did to my hair." A hint of guilt causes my stomach to lurch, but even now, I still don't care for Tim. It might not be too angelic, but I'm still recovering from being human. Plus, I learned Tim will be okay when he leaves this world. So, I don't really feel bad. I add, "What kind of monster does that?"

"Men can be real assholes. I should know," Minx says. "But don't you worry. Doug will take good care of you."

"I'll be there tomorrow at 9:30 a.m. Is that all right?"

"Sure thing. What's the name and number?"

"Robert Snoop," I say. It's a lame name but somehow fitting. I give Minx the phone number of the pay phone and hang up.

I walk away from the phone and blend into the crowd, vanishing. I'm going to need to stop by to leave the money in an envelope, plus something for Minx. That should take care of Doug and should alter his meeting with Tim. I check the ticket, and Tim's phone number fades from the back. On the opposite side, the ticket's timestamp for 9:28 a.m. starts to vanish as well as all the other information. What's left in my hand is a small blank piece of paper. I smile as even the paper vanishes from existence. I give my wings a satisfied flap.

I cross the street, and waiting for me is Fate. He is dressed in his usual black slacks and light-blue dress shirt with the cuffs rolled up. It's a look that suits him. And I can see why Doug found him so appealing.

"Well?" I ask. It's odd to think that all the future, my future, and now my history needed was one missed train, one small event affected so much.

Fate shakes his head. "There will still be death and suffering. Tim's end will not be good. There are a great many deaths to occur because Victoria Hernandez does not rise to power, but she will leave a positive mark on this world. Because of her efforts, a great many things will change for the better. They will take time, but it is as it should be."

I bite my lower lip.

Still more death and pain and nothing I can do.

A hand touches my chin and raises my face. "Let us see what you changed." Fate's warm gaze meets mine.

"I still helped people and made a difference?"

Fate beams down at me. "Why don't you see for yourself." He waves his hand and New York with all its millions of people vanishes.

Chapter Fifteen

I STAND ACROSS the corner, leaning against the stone building as all the people pass. Doug should be along shortly. Today, I'm not here to work, just to observe. Fate has allowed me to watch, to make sure events happen as they should. I promised I would not alter things—*I hope I can keep that promise*. Considering all that has happened and will happen, not much has needed to be repaired. Which is a good feeling, considering I'm the cause of most of the disruption.

Doug turns the corner and peeks up at the big void in the sky. Then uses the building window he was in front of as a mirror to fuss with his spiky blond hair. His nose crinkles, and he distorts his puffy lips into an annoyed expression.

Doug's blond hair was one of my favorite looks. I never did understand his frustrations with his appearance. He was a big guy, even in school, but for some people, that makes them feel safe. I always felt safe around him—like nothing could harm me when he held me tight. Still, Doug, like every other human in every alternate reality, is insecure about how they look. It's a waste of effort, if you ask me. Just be confident and it'll shine through. People are attracted to confidence. A lesson I learned too late.

Ah well.

Doug checks his flip phone and picks up his pace. According to my new knowledge, Doug spent the morning at the memorial site and is now running late for work. *Some things never really change.* I inhale. Doug had always planned on heading to the West Coast, and the attack on 9/11 only made him more desperate to leave, but he didn't have the money yet. It wouldn't be for a couple more years when he got the inheritance from his mother's passing.

Several groups of people pass Doug. He tries to avoid running into any of them and steps out of their way, slowing him down. Finally, he's able to continue walking. He stops again, takes a breath, glances up to where the twin towers once stood, and shakes his head. Several people rush past him again, and he steps out of the way. I follow his gaze and sigh. I understand now I shouldn't have done what I did, but I acted like that for the right reason, and I'm glad Fate didn't have to change it back. Doug quickly wipes his eyes.

I flap my wings and take off. I cross the street and hover slightly above Doug as he moves through the crowds.

"So much suffering and for what?" Doug mumbles. He catches his reflection again and frowns. Doug never saw the beauty just below. Roberto did and will again. I, of course, always saw it. Doug is beautiful, and whatever the outside shows doesn't matter. Not to me or anyone who ever loved him.

I smile as he plays with the spikes of his hair. I love those spikes. They were a lot of fun to play with, and it drove Doug nuts when I messed with them. I chuckle as I watch.

"It's my fault."

I hover back and cast Doug and Tad in a spot of haze, so others don't interfere. I agreed not to make any changes, but I never promised not to help nature take its course. It's an odd feeling watching yourself, even knowing what I know now. I catch the look on Doug's face. I wish I had my smartphone so I could take a picture, but those won't be out for a few years. Not that it matters. It's just a human thought. I get them now and again.

I take in my full appearance on the street. It's bad. I really look awful. Ratty clothes and all the poofy kinky hair. It's dreadful. Even now, I find it difficult to believe Doug took me in, but that goes to show the man's character. He said it was because of Shannon, but I know better. He was always good and kind. He was the one who made things better, even for Shannon.

"I did this," my human double groans. "And now I'm being punished."

"It's not your fault." Doug kneels close to Tad, and I can't help but beam.

I mask them from the rest of the world, just to keep the conversation between them. No one needs to hear this or bother them.

"It was the work of terrorists. They killed all those people, not you." Doug's voice is soft and sweet.

"I should have stopped them. I should have done more," the human me says.

Man, I really am a mess down there. I sigh. There's no need to change this meeting. Without Tim in Doug's life, he would've still stopped, and this was meant to be. A major convergence point, a spot in time that could and should never be changed.

"Oh, baby, no one could have done more." Doug's voice is soft and filled with kindness.

"Now I'm being punished. They sent me here and took my wings," Tad whispers.

"No one is punishing you. Look, it's a tough day for everyone. We all feel like we should have done more." Doug glances over his shoulder. "I've got to get to work." A bright smile fills his face, and his eyes sparkle like jewels. I love that look in his eyes. It always made me feel safe.

"You want to come with me? We'll get you a shower and give you a cut. My girl Minx knows all about your hair type. It'll be fun," Doug says, his voice bubbly and filled with mischief.

He extends his hand.

"You want to help me?" Tad asks, looking around at his filthy surroundings.

Okay, I admit at this point I was a bit of a drama queen. But to be fair, I was living on the streets. I had only been human a year, and let's not forget, my wings had been taken from me. So it sucked. Unless you've experienced it, don't judge.

Doug nods. "Sure. Why not?"

"Most people ignore me. Some people give me money, but they rush by." My doppelganger's voice is filled with surprise.

Oh, Doug, don't. Oh my, there it is. The sniff. Doug falters back.

"Well, not today." Doug dusts off his pants. "I work at a salon near Washington Square. You know it? Anyway, we can walk there and get you all cleaned up. My boss won't mind."

"Thank you," Tad says.

"What's your name?" Doug asks as they walk. I follow above just to make sure nothing new happens. "I'm Doug."

"I don't have a name."

Doug stops and squints. "What?"

"I don't have a name," the human Tad says. "They used to call me..."

I always thought Doug would make fun of me and my story, but he never did. Even later as we got to know each other, he never once laughed at me. I suppose it never mattered to him.

"What?" Doug stops as well. "What did they used to call you? Can't be any worse than what they've called me."

"They used to call me the Angel of Death before they took my wings."

Doug laughs and shakes his head. He looks up, and I have to adjust where I'm watching, or he would be staring right at me. My wings work perfectly, and I float through the air with complete ease.

Doug clears his throat. "Well, we can't call you that. How about Angel?"

Ugh. No. I still don't like that name. My wings shudder.

"Well, I'm not gonna call you *Death,* no matter how cool it sounds." Doug starts to cross the street, ignoring all the strange looks he's getting. At least Doug never cared about how people looked at him or me, especially today.

I have to stop a taxi from almost hitting them. I know I promised not to interfere, but I doubt Fate would mind, especially since Doug was never hit by a taxi that day. The taxi moves on, and Doug is none the wiser. Doug is always clueless to traffic. How he never got hit by a car, when I wasn't around, I won't ever understand.

Look. He continues on like nothing happened.

"You're welcome, Doug," I call out, flapping my wings to hold my position as I watch.

"Oh, I know. How about *Tad*?" Doug says.

"Tad?"

Doug smiles. "Short for 'The Angel of Death.' Well, that would be Taod, but that sounds dumb."

I admit I always liked Tad. I thought the name was clever, and Fate and Death liked it as well.

"Tad it is," Doug says.

They pick up the pace and walk in silence. Doug and Tad reach the shop, and Doug pulls open the door. "Hey, girls, I have a project," he says in his loudest, most over-the-top voice possible. "This is Tad, and we're gonna make him fabulous." He snaps his fingers, and everyone in the shop stares at him.

I chuckle as I pull away. Everything is going to be all right, but there is one more place I need to check. I glance over to Fate, who has joined me, hovering right above Doug, Minx, and the others.

"Can we make another stop?" I ask Fate as he watches. "I have to know for sure. Will that be an issue?"

"No." Fate beams down at me. He flaps his wings and lifts above me toward the heavens.

My wings flutter as I take to the sky, following him.

Chapter Sixteen

DOUG SHIFTED IN bed, hardly able to move. He was short of breath as it had been a challenge to breathe lately. But he realized it wouldn't be for too much longer. His gaze fell to the lush green trees and powder-blue sky out the window. The blinds were raised so he could easily see out. He could almost smell the fresh scent of the recent rain. Several birds flew from the tops of the trees to a new perch, their songs filling the quiet of the day. *It's a beautiful day.* He wheezed out a pleased sigh.

His eyes gently closed as he thought about his home. He was in the room he had shared with Roberto for all their years together. In their bed, as it should be, and as he requested. The heavy rise and fall of his chest a reminder of his advanced age. With his eyes closed, he swore he caught the scent of a meat sauce, with fresh basil and a hint of wine, coming from the kitchen.

All those wonderful meals.

Tad's legendary lasagna. The creamy risottos. Not to be forgotten— the delicious chocolate desserts. Tad was a great cook, just like Shannon. The two had more in common than he ever thought. Not least of all were their green eyes. *I wish they could have known each other.* Another labored sigh exited his lungs. Doug licked at his lips, missing all the wonderful tastes.

"Are you hungry?" a familiar voice asked. "Do you want me to get you something to eat? Soup?"

The edges of his lips pulled up in what he hoped was a smile. "I wish I could have your lasagna."

Tad snickered. "I wish we both could eat rich food again." He cleared his throat, a small cough escaped his lips. "I miss all those amazing times with good food and good friends."

Doug followed the sound and opened his eyes. Tad sat there next to him. His face thin with a sea of wrinkles reflecting a life well-lived. His hair gray and in need of a trim, but his green eyes still as beautiful as the day they met in New York.

Doug tried to shift, but a sharp pain in his hip and chest kept him from moving far, and he bit back a yelp.

"What do you need?" Tad asked.

"Nothing. I'm fine." Doug's voice was weak but determined. *He's being so attentive. I don't want to be a bother. So much like Shannon. Why did I never see it?* So many years in pain. So many years wishing to get better, but now he was ready. He wanted to see his friends again. He wanted to be with Roberto. He wanted to be with Shannon again. And he knew Tad wouldn't mind. "I miss them."

"Of course, you do." Tad's warm breath moved softly over Doug's skin. "We both do."

"I can't believe I'm still here."

"Where else would you be?" Tad brushed Doug's hair off his forehead and then touched his cheek. "You always insisted this is where you wanted to be at the end." Tad removed his hand and beamed down at Doug. "Well, here you are."

"I still don't know how you managed it." Doug used what little strength he had to turn his head closer to Tad's direction. He squinted to see his friend better.

"The magic of the angels." A small chuckle-cough escaped Tad's lips, and for a brief second, he appeared twenty again.

"As beautiful as the day I met you." Doug reached out Tad, but he didn't get far. He was too tired.

Tad took Doug's hand in his. "You flatter me."

"Well, it's true."

Tad's once gentle laugh had a gravelly undertone to it, but it was still a wonderful laugh that continued to raise Doug's spirit and lessen the aches and pains of age.

"I don't know about that." Tad pulled out a handkerchief and swiped at his mouth. "They say ninety is the new seventy, but I don't believe them, especially since I feel every one of my ninety-two years."

"You're not a day over twenty-two, and you know it." Doug coughed and then took a crackly breath. Tad might appear old now, but he wasn't, and Doug finally started to see it. *I wonder why I never saw it before. It has to be some kind of illusion or something.* He tried to laugh but coughed instead.

Doug turned his head and glanced over at the news playing on the wall of his bedroom. He focused on the voice of the TV announcer. "Today, Mars is celebrating its 100,000 population milestone between its two colonies. This news is especially significant as it was only nineteen years ago today that Musk City, then simply referred to as Alpha Base, suffered its worst explosive decompression of the habitat dome." A video image of the explosion played as the newsperson continued to speak. "The disaster of 2051 led to more stringent construction requirements, additional safety and evacuation zones, as well as a push for a full redesign of the carbon nanotubing used in the building of the domes."

Tad peeked at what Doug was watching. "Hard to believe it's been so long. Remember hearing about the accident on the newsfeed."

"It almost threatened the whole planned colony, but Musk pulled it off." Doug shook his head, coughing.

"At least they fixed all the structural issues, and now, Mars is growing. It's amazing they are almost fully self-sufficient." Tad chuckled. "We're finally a space-faring civilization on two different worlds with three space stations and a growing presence on the moon." He sighed. "Amazing."

They both continued to watch the video image as a map showed the new construction of a third base underway. Doug wished he could see Mars. Go there. To be part of building a new world—that would be marvelous. Maybe, even open up a spa. After all, those 100,000 people still needed to look fabulous.

Mars is for the young.

"Do you think Eddie's granddaughter, Elsa, can get the salon there?" Doug took Tad's hand to get his attention.

"I think Elsa will do amazing things." Tad grinned down at their hands, then back at Doug. "You need to stop worrying about what she'll do with the company. You left her a solid foundation to grow and expand." Tad rubbed Doug's hand. "You feel cold. Do you want another blanket?"

"I'm fine." Doug fussed with the blanket covering him, kicking a leg free so it was partially uncovered as he continued to watch the news about Mars.

"They say the people were really lucky. The loss of life could have been much higher." Doug raised his gaze to Tad. "Almost like an angel was watching after them."

"That's what they say." Tad lifted the blanket so he could uncover enough of Doug's leg to keep him happy, but not enough so Doug would get cold. He reached out and sat in his chair.

"Elsa's still a baby." Doug shook his head, trying to focus back on the news. "I can't believe Danielle named her that."

"Why not?" Tad stopped fussing with the blanket and focused on Doug as he talked. "She loved those movies and there are worse names to be called."

"I suppose, and we've been called plenty." Doug carefully adjusted himself on the pillow, trying not to overdo. He took one more look at the images of Mars. "Turn off video feed," he said, and the images vanished as the monitor turned back into a video collage of photos of him with Roberto, Minx, Paul, Eddie, Tad, and everyone from his life. There was even a smattering of images of Shannon. Doug had had to dig for them, but he had found them. "You know there was a time in the 2020s I didn't think we would make it this far." He took a breath. "Kind of like a bad dream, with a war and bombs." He shuddered. "It felt so real. But it wasn't, was it?"

"No, I suppose not."

Doug narrowed his gaze on Tad. "You did it, didn't you? You made sure we were all safe, and you helped the people on Mars. I never believed you were an angel, but I know better now."

"You need to rest." Tad grinned.

"Fine, don't tell me." Doug cleared his throat before sighing. "With Roberto gone, I'm glad you're here."

Tad adjusted how he was sitting in the chair, pulling himself closer to Doug. He took Doug's hand again.

"Saying goodbye to Roberto after forty years wasn't easy, but we had the best life together, and I wouldn't change any of it."

"I'm glad."

Doug had outlived a majority of friends including Minx, but that queen managed to go out in style with a massive heart attack in full drag while performing onstage for a one-off show of all their drag sisters from the turn of the century. Doug closed his eyes, picturing Minx up onstage giving it her all. *She wouldn't have had it any other way.* He only wished he could have seen Minx more in their later years.

Now it was just Doug and Tad. Somehow, Doug had known it would be his time sooner rather than later. He didn't mind; he had everything he needed right here, and that was wonderful.

"Did you have a happy life?" Tad gave Doug's hand another squeeze.

"Of course. You were there for me all these years. I loved every minute of it." Doug's breath became more labored and his words were slower. "Even when you didn't know who you were." His voice grew softer. "We had a blast and everyone loved us." He coughed again. "I had the perfect guardian angel."

"I'm not a guardian angel. I'm your friend."

There was a flapping sound, and Doug squinted toward the bedroom door. A shape casually materialized. A grin filled Doug's face. "I remember you." He raised a shaky hand and pointed to the female Angel of Death. "How could I ever forget those beautiful almond-shaped eyes and your saucy black hair?"

"I said I was keeping my eye on you." She winked, crossed over to Tad, and rested a hand on his shoulder.

Tad released Doug's hand and stood. He bowed his head and stepped to the side so she could pass.

The Angel of Death stood there with Tad. Tad shook his shoulders, and the old man with the beautiful green eyes gradually vanished. The frail frame of age was now gone, revealing a man he hadn't seen in seventy years. The broad shoulders, defined chest, and slim waist all returned. Tad's bright-white wings glowed in the light of the room, a stunning contrast to his cocoa skin.

"I always knew you were an angel." Doug reached up.

Tad's face filled with a bright smile, and he stepped nearer the window.

Behind Tad, at the window, was another man who appeared and rested a hand on Tad's shoulder. It was Fate.

"It's been many years, Doug," Fate said. "I hope your life was all you wanted it to be. Never a wasted moment."

"It's been everything and more." Doug coughed.

Fate nodded and glanced over at Tad. "It's time." Fate squeezed Tad's shoulder.

Tad nodded and stepped forward. He beamed over at Doug.

Doug watched through half-closed lids as Tad shut his eyes and lowered his head. It only took a moment, but everything Tad was melted away in a warm glow that caused Doug to raise a shaky hand to cover his eyes.

The angelic glow faded and Doug lowered his hand. A young man stepped forward. "Hi, Dougy." The soft effeminate voice of the young man was nothing like Tad's. He had a soft lisp, one Doug recognized in an instant.

"Shannon. It's you, but how?" Doug blinked several times and pinched the bridge of his nose.

The young man played with his hands and nibbled at his lower lip. "I'm sorry I hid who I was from you."

"I thought only Archangels could change their appearance." Doug asked as more of the memories from his encounters with the angels returned to his slowing mind.

The boy continued to play with his hands in front of him. He peeked over at Fate.

"That's not completely true." Fate offered a lopsided smile. "However, I did assist Tad, or as you see him here, Shannon, with his other form."

Doug's face warmed, and he took a shaky breath. "Has it always been you?"

Shannon gnawed at his lower lip. "I couldn't leave you like that." His gaze dropped to the floor. "That night at prom. I was so angry and so selfish." He took another step forward. "I was an awfully self-centered person, even during my second chance at being human, but you only ever saw the good in me. I should have learned. I'm sorry. Please, can you forgive me for all the hurt and pain I caused you?" He quickly wiped at his eyes.

"Oh, my beautiful boy," Doug coughed. "I hated what you did, but I understood. I always thought you were too good for this world, and I know now I was right." Doug shifted his gaze over to Fate. "Thank you, Fate, for watching after him. You have no idea what this means to me." Doug reached out his time-weathered hand. It shook and ached but was fine. He was fine. Or he soon would be. "You don't have to apologize, not to me. Never to me."

"No, I was wrong." Shannon's voice grew louder. "I let them win. I gave the bullies the power over me. But I had the power, and I gave it to them—I let them hurt me. I let them win, and that was wrong." His face and neck started to redden.

Doug tried not to smile; he was starting to understand, and his heart was slowly growing lighter. His old friend stood before him, trying to explain all the hurt and anger he must have felt that day, but for Doug, it was so long ago, and he was seeing his friend for the first time in all those years. He had forgotten how waifish Shannon was—all it would take was a strong wind and he would probably blow away.

"I wanted them all to hurt as much as me," Shannon said. "But the only one I hurt was you...well, and my family, but I've made peace with them. Now it's you."

Doug forced himself to sit forward, the pained grin never leaving his face. "You did let them win, and you only hurt those who loved you most, but I could never be mad at you, especially now."

"Thank you." Shannon licked his lips.

Doug watched him start to reach for the glass of water on the side table, but he stopped. Shannon shook his head and glanced up to the Angel of Death and to Fate. "For my penance..."

Fate returned a hand to Shannon's shoulder.

Doug waited. He understood how all this was important, not only to Shannon but to the two of them and their long lives.

Shannon took a breath. "When I was offered this chance, I knew I had to take it." He peered over his shoulder at Fate again, who smiled and nodded. "To make up for all the hurt I caused and to learn about life and living."

"You were an amazing man and friend as Tad." Doug tried to shift on the bed but found his body was barely responding anymore. "I'm just glad you're here. I know you're safe and well."

Shannon reached out, took Doug's hand, and gave it a squeeze.

"My beautiful Shannon." Doug beamed up at Shannon. "You make an amazing angel."

"I'm sorry I had to deceive you. I didn't really know who I was until Fate returned for me, so it's not really a lie." Shannon offered a hint of a playful grin, one Doug hadn't seen since they were boys. Shannon sat on the bed next to Doug.

Doug laughed.

"As far as surprises go, I don't mind this one." Doug tried to lean over but couldn't, so Shannon leaned in to Doug, hugging him.

"It's time," Death's easygoing voice said. She stepped forward and reached out to take both Doug's and Shannon's hands.

She nodded toward Shannon, who got up and stepped back. Shannon's hand released Doug's. He was left with only the warm hand of Death. She winked at him, leaned in, and kissed his forehead.

A warm sense of peace started from her kiss and traveled through Doug's body. He closed his eyes as the sensations reached every part of him. The warmth filled him. He was no longer tired. He was ready to get up and move. To be free of all the aches and pains.

SHANNON GLANCED AT the hand of his teacher resting again on his shoulder and then to his sister as she took care of Doug. They had done it. The world was as it should be. Everything was set right, and Doug got the life he was meant to have. Shannon could ask for no more.

Through all the years of being Tad, he had learned a great deal, but nothing as important as to love and to be brave. Yes, there was heartache and pain, but that was life, a human life. And he got to experience it. He wasn't perfect, but no human was, and he wondered if that was part of what he was meant to learn.

There were several yips at their feet.

Shannon peeked down. "Hiya, Snoop."

Shannon glanced at Death as she stepped back, still holding Doug's hand and lifting him from the bed. Death moved to the side, and Doug continued forward.

There was another yip from the bouncy dog at their feet.

"She waited for me." Doug followed Shannon's gaze.

"She waited for the both of you at the Rainbow Bridge." Fate rested a hand on each of their shoulders.

Shannon leaned down and picked her up, cradling her in his arms as she licked his face. She was little more than a puppy, perhaps a year old. "I'm so glad we found her."

"You always did love dogs." Doug rubbed Snoopy's head as she licked his hand.

"My parents never wanted me to have a pet," Shannon said, but the smile didn't leave his face. There was no anger anymore. Shannon's past with his parents was a fact of his life, of the life before Tad. "My folks said having a dog was too much work, but after they passed I got to introduce them to Snoopy and they loved her. It all seems so silly and unimportant now." He beamed down at Snoopy.

Doug fussed with the blond spikes. He stopped for a moment. "My spikes are back."

Death nodded. "Of course, you are your most glorious self."

Doug played around with his hair.

"You may look back at yourself, if you wish." The Angel of Death's voice was gentle. "But understand, what's left in the bed isn't you. It's just window dressing, a shell of what you were. You're free from all that now, at peace and whole." Her beautiful almond eyes focused on Doug, then turned to Shannon. "However, some people like to look back."

"I only want to move forward." Doug reached for Shannon's hand.

Shannon took Doug's in his. Even in this state, just holding his hand sent a shiver through every part of his body, and his heart skipped a beat.

"Shannon, are you ready to join Doug?" Fate asked, pointing to where the window had been only moment ago. Before them was nothing but warmth and light.

"I can go with him? What about Roberto? What about being an Angel of Death?" Shannon asked.

"What you do next is up to you." Fate nodded. "As for Roberto, I believe he will be pleased to see you. Remember, brother, there is no jealousy, only peace and joy."

Tad nodded and glanced down at Doug's hand. His moved up to Doug's young handsome face. "I've never been beyond the veil."

"There is much still to learn and see." Fate pointed. "You've learned all I can teach, and your services as an Angel of Death are no longer required. You have done well, my brother. However, if you wish to remain an Angel of Death, I would be pleased to have you."

"As would I, brother." The female Angel of Death reached her hand out to Shannon.

He faced Doug and stared at the path of light and warmth ahead. "I want to only move forward."

M.D. NEU
Author

THANK YOU!

Your opinion counts:

I hope you enjoyed my novel.

If you get a chance, please help me and potential readers by writing a book review on Amazon.

Readers rely on reader reviews to make book purchases so your feedback is valued.

To share your review on Amazon:
1. Log into your Amazon account > Search for my book
2. Click on 'customer reviews'
3. Click on 'write customer review' and share your thoughts

Thank you for your support!

SUBSCRIBE

Enjoy what you're reading?

Want to keep up to date with new releases and special events?

Subscribe today to my website for weekly updates and special announcements.

Visit my website at *www.mdneu.com* and hit the **contact/subscribe** button.

Want to join the conversation, follow me on social media.

M.D. NEU
www.mdneu.com

Acknowledgements

I've known angels throughout my life and I believe they are with us always, even if we can't see them.

As always, I need to thank my amazing beta readers for all their help with this story. There was a lot I needed to get right with this story so their help was invaluable. Also, I have to include warm hugs to my amazing husband, family, and friends. None of this would be possible without them.

About the Author

M.D. Neu is an LGBTQA fiction writer with a love for writing and travel. Living in the heart of Silicon Valley (San Jose, California) and growing up around technology, he's always been fascinated with what could be. Specifically drawn to sci-fi and paranormal television and novels, M.D. Neu was inspired by the great Gene Roddenberry, George Lucas, Stephen King, Alice Walker, Alfred Hitchcock, Harvey Fierstein, Anne Rice, and Kim Stanley Robinson. An odd combination, but one that has influenced his writing.

Growing up in an accepting family as a gay man, he always wondered why there were never stories reflecting who he was. Constantly surrounded by characters that only reflected heterosexual society, M.D. Neu decided he wanted to change that. So, he took to writing, wanting to tell good stories that reflected our diverse world.

When M.D. Neu isn't writing, he works for a nonprofit and travels with his biggest supporter and his harshest critic, Eric, his husband of nineteen plus years.

Email: info@mdneu.com

Facebook: www.facebook.com/mdneuauthor

Twitter: @Writer_MDNeu

Website: www.mdneu.com

Instagram: www.instagram.com/authormdneu

Blog: www.mdneu.com/blog

Other books by this author

The Calling
The Reunion
A Dragon for Christmas
Contact, A New World, book one
Conviction, A New World, book two

Also Available from NineStar Press

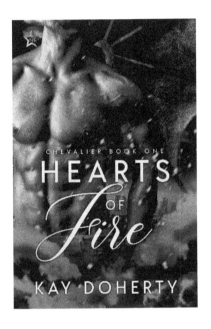

Connect with NineStar Press

www.ninestarpress.com

www.facebook.com/ninestarpress

www.facebook.com/groups/NineStarNiche

www.twitter.com/ninestarpress

www.tumblr.com/blog/ninestarpress

CPSIA information can be obtained
at www.ICGtesting.com
Printed in the USA
FSHW010138170919
62083FS